AUTHOR IN THE ETHER

Warrick had to solve this mystery, discover how to gain mastery over the power of the strange device and the unknown adept who had created it. He could think of nothing else. He was obsessed.

"I am *not* obsessed," said the troll.

"I said, 'I'm not obsessed.'"

"Master, I said nothing!" the troll protested.

"Come to think of it," said Warrick with a frown, "I heard nothing. But there *was* a voice. I ... sensed it."

The troll's eyes grew wide.

"It's talking about your eyes now," Warrick said. He glanced at the time machine. "Things have been peculiar since that time machine came into my possession."

"*Time machine*, master?"

"What?"

"You said, 'time machine.'"

"I did, didn't I? I wonder what it means? And I wonder how I knew to call it that."

"Perhaps the voice told you," offered the troll.

"The ... voice," said Warrick. "I sense a presence ... an omniscient presence ..."

++

THE RELUCTANT SORCERER

Also by Simon Hawke

THE WIZARD OF 4TH STREET
THE WIZARD OF WHITECHAPEL
THE WIZARD OF SUNSET STRIP
THE WIZARD OF RUE MORGUE
SAMURAI WIZARD
THE WIZARD OF SANTA FE

THE RELUCTANT SORCERER

SIMON HAWKE

WARNER BOOKS

A Time Warner Company

WARNER BOOKS EDITION

Copyright © 1992 by Simon Hawke
All rights reserved.

Cover design by Don Puckey
Cover illustration by Dave Mattingly

Warner Books, Inc.
1271 Avenue of the Americas
New York, N.Y. 10020

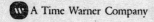 A Time Warner Company

Printed in the United States of America

First Printing: May, 1992

10 9 8 7 6 5 4 3 2 1

This one's for you, Yang...

The author wishes to acknowledge the contributions of a group of people known as The Mad Scientists, many of whom acted as technical advisors on *The Reluctant Sorcerer*.

Special thanks to C. Pat McGivney and Jane Labie-McGivney, Mike Bakula, Bill Lemieux, Bruce Miller, Sandy Diersing, Bob Pfeifer, Jay Bohmer, Rachel Drummond, John and Bonnie Doran, Fred Cleaver, Claude N. Warren, Jr., John Morse, Charles Harrison, Bill Llewellin (got it right this time, Bill), Paula Johnson, David Gibbons, Christyna Ivers, Doug Lott, Cheryl Green, Charlotte Taylor, Mary Heller, Leanne Christine Harper, Ed Bryant, Adele Leone, the members of the Denver Area Science Fiction Association, Megan McDowell, Robert Asprin, Robert M. Powers, Harlan Ellison (not that you did anything, Harlan, but "just because you're you"), Frank Frazetta, whose art inspired Black Shannon, Dave Mattingly, a constant inspiration, and Brian Thomsen, who got me thinking along these lines in the first place and maybe now doesn't wish to be held responsible. A very special debt must be acknowledged to the late Jay Ward, who subverted an entire generation and whose like will not be seen again. And to Jeffrey C. Kraus, the original "voice in the aether," who taught me much. If I hadn't worked on "Sterling Bronson," I may never have written this.

CHAPTER
O N E

"It's alive! It's alive!"

"Darling . . . come to bed."

"Just a minute," replied Marvin Brewster, staring raptly at the television set where Colin Clive, in the role of Dr. Victor Frankenstein, was gripped in a paroxysm of unholy glee as his creation twitched to life on the laboratory table.

"Darling . . ." Her voice was low and throaty with a British accent. "I'm waiting . . ."

"Ummm." Brewster didn't turn around. If he had, he would have seen a sight that would have reduced most men to drooling idiots. His fiancée, Dr. Pamela Fairburn, was standing in the bedroom doorway, dressed in nothing but a slinky negligee that was so sheer, it looked like a soft mist enveloping her lush, voluptuous curves. She stood in a pose of calculated seduction, one long and lovely leg bent at the knee, one arm stretched out above her, pressed against the door frame, her long auburn hair worn loose and cascading down to her ample, perfumed cleavage. . . .

Whoa, wait a minute. Let me catch my breath.

Sorry about that. Narrators are only human too, you

1

know. Okay, now where were we? Oh, right. This gorgeous, incredibly desirable woman is exuding premarital lust all over the place and that fool, Brewster, is simply sitting there and watching a monster movie on TV. Any other red-blooded male would know exactly what to do, right? You betcha. Hit that remote control and make a beeline for the bedroom. Any normal, sensible man hearing that incredibly sultry and seductive voice would turn around, take one look, and experience the hormonal equivalent of a nuclear meltdown. (And considering how beautiful Dr. Pamela Fairburn was, a lot of women would, as well.) However, Dr. Marvin Brewster was not exactly normal. Or sensible. That is to say, he was incredibly intelligent—a genius, in fact—but he didn't have a lot of street smarts.

Nor was this just any movie. To Marvin Brewster, it was *the* movie, the one that had the single most significant impact on his formative years. The one that had made him realize exactly what he wanted to be when he grew up. He first saw it at the age of nine and from that moment on, he *knew*. He was going to be a mad scientist.

It wasn't Boris Karloff's portrayal of the monster that had so affected him, nor the idea of creating life from sewn-together pieces of dead bodies, it was that laboratory. All that marvelous equipment. The bubbling vials and beakers, the intricate plumbing and wiring, the spinning dials, the Jacob's ladder arcing electrical current. . . . He took one look at that wonderful laboratory and he fell in love, a love far deeper and more abiding than he would ever feel for any woman, even a woman as undeniably womanly as Pamela Fairburn.

She knew and understood this. Earlier that evening, when she had spotted the listing for the film, she'd realized what was liable to happen and she had hidden the *TV Guide*, but Brewster had just happened to turn on the tube after their late-night dinner, and scanning through the channels, he'd stumbled on the film. Now Pamela knew there'd be no prying him away till it was over.

She sighed with resignation and walked over to the couch where he was sitting, settled down onto the floor beside him, and leaned her head against his knee. Without turning from the television, he offered her the bowl of popcorn. She took a handful and popped it in her mouth. Even in her sexiest lingerie, she knew she couldn't compete. She didn't really mind, however. She understood about obsession. She had one of her own, and that was her career as a cybernetics engineer, which was how she had met Brewster.

It had been during a symposium at Cambridge. She'd spotted him at once. He was the only American present, but that wasn't what had made him stand out. There was just something about him, about his rumpled, tweedy, and horn-rimmed appearance, his curly and unkempt blond hair, his rather shambling and distracted manner, and his total unself-consciousness that had struck her as incredibly endearing. He was part little boy, part unmade bed. He had gotten to her where she lived, where most women live, in fact. Right smack in her maternal instinct. She wanted to pull him to her breast and hug him to pieces.

She was later to discover that Brewster often had that effect on women and part of his charm was that he was totally oblivious to it. He was simply clueless. He was the kind of man women wanted to mother into bed, only he was so preoccupied and absentminded that if they succeeded, he would probably forget why he was there. Pamela Fairburn could have had any man she wanted. She could walk into a crowded room and every man present would immediately go on point. All she'd need to do to insure most men's undying and slavish devotion would be to flutter her eyelashes and act stupid. But with Marvin Brewster, she could be herself.

Her intelligence did not intimidate him. More often than not, it was the other way around. She could talk about her work with him, and he could easily follow the discussion and make acute and often brilliant observations, but then his eyes would suddenly go dreamy and he'd launch into a flight of technical verbosity that would leave her absolutely breathless as his words tumbled over one another until he became hopelessly tongue-tied and had to resort to scribbling complicated equations on whatever surface was available. Even on the rare occasions when she was able to make out his cramped scrawl, most of the time she could make no sense of it.

Often, it was because his mind simply worked so quickly that it would outrace his written calculations and he'd leave things out, jumping on ahead, with no awareness that she couldn't follow him. His brain would simply shift into warp speed and he would rocket off into that rarified atmosphere where only geniuses and angels fly and he'd finish off with a triumphant, *"There,* you see?" And, of course, she wouldn't see at all, but she would simply stare at him, eyes shining, and she would say, "I love you."

They became engaged one year after their first meeting. She had proposed to him, primarily because she'd realized the thought would never have occurred to him. He needed her, but he was simply too preoccupied to notice. The ordinary details of everyday life were not Marvin Brewster's strong point. He was the classic absentminded professor. His socks hardly ever matched. He wore loafers because he would often forget to tie his shoelaces. He was simply hopeless about clothes. Until she came along, he was dressed by an understanding local haberdashery. He would come in and simply say, "I need some ties," or a sport coat or a shirt or two, and the helpful female sales clerk would pick out something appropriate for him.

It was the same with groceries. There was a young woman who managed the local market who would call from time to time and say, "Dr. Brewster? This is Sheila. You haven't been in for a while and I thought you might be running out." And he would walk over to the refrigerator or the cupboard, stare into it absently for a moment or two, then say distractedly, "Yes, I suppose I must be." Sheila would then take the shopping cart around during her lunch break, pick out his groceries for him, and have them delivered. He never had to pay for them, either. The branch manager at the local bank, also an attractive young woman, had seen to it that he had accounts everywhere and that the bills were sent directly to the bank.

The multinational conglomerate that employed Brewster for an astronomical salary (that was still a pittance compared to the profits they took in from the dozen or so patents he'd turned over to them) always deposited his checks directly into his accounts, so that Brewster never had to deal with the various mundane tasks of shopping and record keeping and checkbook balancing that plague most lesser mortals.

How does one get a deal like this? The answer is, one doesn't. It's not the sort of thing you can manage to arrange, unless you happen to be born with a certain indefinable and helpless charm that women find simply irresistible. Ask any woman in London who knows him how she feels about Dr. Marvin Brewster, and whether she's sixteen or sixty, she'll sigh and her eyes will get all soft and misty and she'll say, "He's such a *dear* man. . . ."

When Pamela discovered just how many women felt this way about her intended, she became a bit alarmed. She seized the reins and took firm control of Marvin Brewster's life. If there was any mothering to be done here, by God, *she* was going to be the one to do it! She moved in on

Marvin Brewster like Grant moved in on Richmond. Now all she had to do was figure out how to get him to the altar. He had already missed three scheduled weddings.

The first time she'd been left waiting at the altar, the wedding had completely slipped his mind and a frantic search that included a check of half the pubs and all the hospitals in London eventually found him deep in the stacks of the science library—about eight hours too late. The second time, once again, all the guests arrived, and Pamela once more donned her wedding gown, and once again, no Brewster. This time, he had driven off to Liverpool, to an electronics warehouse, to pick up some obscure part for a piece of lab equipment that was "absolutely vital" and somehow he got sidetracked and no one saw or heard anything from him for two days. The last time—"Shall we try for three?" the minister had wryly asked—they located him in his high-security, private laboratory high atop the corporate headquarters building of EnGulfCo International, only no one could get in past the retinal pattern scanner and they couldn't even take the elevator up to the right floor because the special palm scanner pad would only respond to Marvin Brewster's hand. They had called and called, but Brewster had been distracted by the ringing of the phone, and absentmindedly, he had simply turned it off. The last time, when the wedding invitations were sent out, most of the guests sent back their regrets and their assurances that they would be with them in spirit—*whenever* they finally got around to getting married. Pamela's father still wasn't speaking to her. Still, she was undaunted. One of these days, she'd get it done, only it would require proper planning. Perhaps next time she'd hire some security guards to baby-sit him and deliver him to church on time.

She sat there with him, munching popcorn while Boris Karloff lumbered through the film in his built-up boots and makeup, and during the commercials, Brewster would become absorbed in double-, triple-, and quadruple-checking some kind of circuit board and switch assembly he had put together on the coffee table.

Perhaps, thought Pamela, if she got pregnant, she could command more of his attention. Marvin was always wonderful with children. Probably because, in many ways, he was still something of a child himself, she thought with a smile. The children in the neighborhood all idolized him, and like most of Brewster's friends, they called him Doc. Pamela drew the line at that. She never called him Doc, it seemed too flippant. But whenever she introduced him as Dr. Marvin Brewster, he would invariably add, "But my friends all call me Doc." When they were finally married, she would put a stop to that. A man of his position needed to be treated with proper respect.

What did Brewster think of all this planning for his future? Actually, he gave it very little thought at all. He was more concerned with the past. Not his own past, but the past in general. As in time. Specifically, as in time travel.

He did not really discuss this particular obsession with his fiancée, nor with his colleagues, because as any good mad scientist knows, when you get into the sort of stuff that "man was not meant to know," you're simply asking for trouble. It was one thing for theoretical physicists to debate whether or not Einstein was right, and to play all sorts of fanciful games (often in science fiction novels) with hyperspace and warps in the space/time continuum, but when you actually came out and said that you could *do* it, and revealed a working prototype, that was when they broke out the torches and the pitchforks.

No, Marvin Brewster would not make Dr. Victor Frankenstein's mistake. First he'd do it and make absolutely sure it worked, and then he would publish and take out the patent, which EnGulfCo would at once appropriate, since he'd done it on their premises and with their funding, but that was fine, Brewster didn't really mind that. The money he would make would not be insignificant and money wasn't really what the whole thing was about. Proving Einstein wrong. *That* was what the whole thing was about.

If it had seemed to Pamela that Brewster was much more than typically preoccupied during the past month or two, and letting little things (such as the occasional wedding) slip his mind, then it was because Brewster was wrestling with a problem that had him on the threshold, as it were, of the greatest achievement of his life.

High atop the corporate headquarters building of EnGulfCo International, in his top secret laboratory where no one else, not even the EnGulfCo CEO, could gain admittance, Marvin Brewster had built himself a time machine.

H. G. Wells would have been proud. It even *looked* right. About the size of a small helicopter, the front of the machine was dominated by a plastic bubble that had, in fact, been lifted from a chopper. It had a door in its left side, edged by a pressure seal, and the frame of the machine was also taken from a helicopter, so that it sat on skids. Brewster had replaced the gearbox with high-power alternators and a turboshaft engine, mounted vertically. The intake for the turbine extended out the top of the machine and just behind it was a can for a ballistic parachute. The back of the machine also housed the tanks for fuel and liquid oxygen and environmental gas. Flanking the power systems were the primary capacitor banks, housed in two cabinets on the sides of the machine.

Externally, the time machine did not appear much different from a helicopter with the rotor blades and tail removed, except for one particular, distinguishing feature. Encircling the entire assembly and the frame, positioned diagonally so that it ran around the top of the bubble and behind the back skids, was a stainless-steel tube three inches in diameter, a torus encircled by loops of superconducting wire, the interior of which was filled with a small amount of a rare substance known by the innocuous name of Buckyballs.

Not just anyone could play with Buckyballs. The existence of this substance had first been postulated by Buckminster Fuller (hence, the name) and it was, in fact, an incredibly dense black powder composed of a single atom of iron surrounded by diamond, the ash from a supernova. Its density rendered it extremely heavy. A mere handful weighed about two hundred pounds. It was magnetic and completely frictionless. Needless to say, this wasn't the sort of stuff one could pick up at the local Radio Shack. In fact, one couldn't really pick it up at all without a forklift. It sort of had to fall into one's hands—like, from outer space—which this particular batch had done, contained inside a meteor, a small piece of an asteroid that had been floating around in the Big Empty for a length of time that had more zeroes in it than even Carl Sagan could imagine.

Brewster got his hands on this stuff with some difficulty. The meteor in question had fallen on a small Pacific Island that now had one *very* large hole. It had wiped out a small village, and a number of small villagers who were descended from a group of canoe-worshipers that had settled on this island some three thousand years ago and lived there in abject poverty and squalor ever since. One of their legends had it that someday their wealth would fall from the skies. It did. Now the survivors of this windfall were all living in luxury apartments and driving Mercedes-Benz convertibles. This had, needless to say, cost EnGulfCo quite a bundle, but they figured that if Brewster needed this stuff, chances were that he was onto something that was liable to be very profitable in the not-too-distant future. In the meantime, they had obtained exclusive offshore drilling rights.

What made this substance special was that if it was started spinning on the inside of the tube, with magnetic coils preventing it from contacting the sides, somewhat like in a cyclotron, theory had it that if the Buckyballs went fast enough, at the speed approaching that of light, it would create a warp in space/time. And whatever was inside the field would drop through.

To where? Good question. This was what Brewster intended to find out. You see, he had done this before. A couple of times, in fact. The first time traveler in history was a lop-eared rabbit Brewster had purchased in a pet shop and named Bugs. (What else?) The experiment that Brewster had set up went something like this:

(Actually, it went *exactly* like this, but it's complicated, so pay close attention.) He placed Bugs inside a cage and then he placed the cage inside the time machine, which he then programmed to travel back in time ten minutes for ten seconds. Before he did this, he used a forklift (which he'd needed for the Buckyballs, remember?) to move the time machine about fifteen feet to one side, so that when it appeared ten minutes in the past, it would not appear on the exact same spot where it had been sitting earlier. (Confusing? Wait. It gets worse.)

Theoretically (that is, assuming it all worked), Brewster should have wound up with two time machines sitting side by side, about fifteen feet apart. Now, this might seem like something of a paradox, since if he sent the machine back ten minutes into the past, then it should have made the journey and appeared ten minutes *before* it had ever left. Which meant that there would be *two* time machines and *two* lop-eared rabbits named Bugs sitting on the floor of

Brewster's laboratory ten minutes before he'd ever sent the first one back.

But . . . wait a minute. That doesn't make sense. (At least, not logically, which doesn't necessarily have anything to do with temporal physics, but let's not get into that right now, because you're probably confused enough.) Before Brewster sent the machine back into the past, there had to *be* a past in which he hadn't sent it back at all. The moment that he sent it back, he would, in effect, have altered history. At least *his* history, which meant that the moment he programmed the machine and tripped the switch to send it back ten minutes for ten seconds, at the very instant that it disappeared, he should have suddenly acquired a memory of standing in the lab and seeing two time machines, standing side by side. At least, that's how he *thought* it would work. He was not exactly sure. But then, in scientific experiments, one never is, is one?

The problem was, that wasn't how it worked in practice. What happened was that Brewster had programmed the machine, entered the auto-return sequence, and tripped the timer switch to send it back. And it had disappeared. Only Brewster did *not* suddenly acquire a memory of having seen two time machines sitting side by side, ten minutes earlier. The machine had simply disappeared, complete with Bugs, and reappeared on the exact same spot ten seconds later. Where had it been? Brewster had no way of knowing. He had repeated the experiment with more or less the same results.

This posed certain problems. Did this mean that there was a sort of linear factor to time, where there was now a past in which Brewster *had*, in fact, seen a pair of time machines sitting side by side, complete with two rabbit passengers, but he could not remember it because he only had that experience further back along the timestream? And since he had repeated the experiment, did this suggest that there were now *two* past segments of the timestream, one in which he had seen two time machines and two rabbits, and another, slightly further back, in which he had seen three time machines and three rabbits? The whole thing gave Brewster quite a headache. (And if you feel like putting down the book right now and taking a couple of aspirin, your narrator doesn't mind at all. Go ahead. I'll wait.)

The only solution to this dilemma that Brewster could devise was to actually get inside the time machine himself, so that he could find out where it went after he tripped the switch. (A video camera might have been an excellent solution to this problem, but he had tried that and discovered that the temporal field caused interference.) He had actually planned to make the trip himself all along, though he would have liked having some solid data before he made the attempt. However, Bugs seemed none the worse for wear after his two journeys, so Brewster felt the risk was justified. After all, nothing ventured, nothing gained.

He had set everything up again, carefully following the same procedure, and he had programmed in the sequence, complete with auto-return commands. He had then set the timer, and turned around to pick up his notepad and his pen before getting into the machine . . . only when he turned around again, the thing had disappeared. The trouble was, this time, it did not come back. This was why Brewster had been so distracted during the past two months, while Pamela had been trying to get him to the church. She wanted him to say ''I do,'' only he kept repeating, ''I don't get it.''

The first time he had missed the wedding, he'd been sequestered in the library, combing through the work of Albert Einstein to see if maybe there was something he'd missed. There wasn't. The second time he blew it, when he'd made the trip to Liverpool, he had gone to pick up the special microchip component that would allow him to assemble several more circuit boards for the auto-return modules, so he could run tests to see where the thing might have malfunctioned. The third time, the occasion of Pamela's breakdown in communications with her father, he'd been locked up in the lab, putting the circuit boards together and assembling the modules. And so far as he could tell, there were no problems in the wiring or the assembly.

He found the whole experience extremely frustrating and he had taken to carrying at least one of the modules around with him, taking it apart and putting it back together again repeatedly, running tests and scratching his head and generally being off in the ozone somewhere, which Pamela found rather trying. However, she was a patient woman and she knew that as soon as Brewster managed to clear up whatever problem was presently occupying his attention, there would be a space of time, however short, in which he would be receptive to new ideas. Such as getting married, for instance. So Pamela didn't press. But the moment he worked out whatever it was that he was working on, she was going to pounce.

The commercial ended and Brewster set the little black box that he had reassembled back down on the coffee table. Almost absently, he tripped a little switch on it. And an instant after he did it, it quietly clicked back to its original position.

"*Damn!*" Brewster suddenly exclaimed, leaping to his feet and sending popcorn tumbling all over the rug and Pamela's hair. "*That's it!*"

"*Marvin!*" Pamela protested, brushing greasy kernels of unpopped corn out of her hair, but Brewster was already rushing across the room and flinging open the front door of their apartment. "Marvin, where are you going? *Marvin!* Your *shoes!*"

The door slammed shut behind him. She sighed heavily. A moment later he came barging back in his stocking feet, swept up his brown tasseled loafers, pecked her on the cheek, and said, "I've just got to check this out, dear, but it may take a while. Love you. Don't wait up."

"Marvin..."

But he'd stormed out again, carrying the little black box under his arm, only this time forgetting to close the door behind him.

"Oh, Marvin..." she said. With an air of resignation, she got up and closed the door. She was more or less accustomed to this sort of thing, but this time, whatever it was that had been frustrating him so, he must have gotten it licked, because he had run out in the middle of the movie, and he'd never done *that* before.

"Don't wait up," he'd said. Like hell she wouldn't wait up. If it took all night, she'd wait for him to return, doubtless brimming over with enthusiasm over whatever gadget it was that he'd finally managed to get working, wanting to tell her all about it. She would sit there and she'd listen and she'd share his pleasure and *then*, when he stopped to catch his breath (by then it would be dawn, most likely), she would put a tie and freshly laundered shirt on him, take him by the hand, and lead him down the nearest aisle she could find.

She picked up a handful of spilled popcorn from the carpet and popped it in her mouth, then glanced at the clock atop the mantelpiece. Almost two A.M. It was late.

Too late, in fact.

Brewster rode the elevator up to his private laboratory atop the corporate headquarters building of EnGulfCo International, all the while thinking, God, it was so *simple!*

A faulty counter in the timing switch, that was all it was.

He was certain of it. He had tried everything else that he could think of in an attempt to reproduce the malfunction that had sent the first time machine off on the journey from which it had never returned and now he was certain that he had it. Everything else had checked out perfectly, with each and every one of the duplicate circuit boards for the auto-return module he had assembled, but this one had a faulty timing switch. The moment he tripped it, instead of the counter sequentially going backward from "30" to "0," the settings he'd selected, it went from "30" *directly* to "0," without going through all the numbers in between, so no sooner had he tripped the switch than it clicked back again to its original position. That must have been what happened with the original machine. Some of the switches had been faulty and the auto-return had simply turned itself off an instant after he'd activated it. Damned English electronics, he thought, should have gone with Japanese components. No wonder the damn thing hadn't come back. It had departed on a one-way trip!

He passed the scanner and entered his laboratory, where the second time machine, the one he'd painstakingly recreated during the past two months, sat waiting in the center of the room. He stood there for a moment, staring at it and chewing on his lower lip. He *had* to be right this time. He'd used up the very last of the Buckyballs in putting the second one together. If it didn't work right this time, that would be the end of it, at least until another obliging meteor containing fragments of a supernova from some other galaxy happened to smack into some unsuspecting piece of earthly real estate. And that could take a while.

"It has to work this time," he mumbled to himself, "it *has* to!"

Just to make sure, he double-, triple-, and quadruple-checked all the other switches for the duplicate auto-return modules he had assembled. He found two more that had the same malfunction, but all the others worked properly.

"That's it," he said to himself. "That's *got* to be it."

So simple. He had thought something had gone wrong in the assembly of the board, and he had done it over and over and over again, and all the time, it had just been a faulty switch.

He rechecked all the working switches several more times, just to make certain, then he selected one and snapped the module into the control panel. That's all there was to it.

"*Now,*" he said. He turned to look at Bugs, sitting in his wire cage, looking fat and healthy and munching contentedly on a piece of lettuce. "Now we find out where you've been off to, Bugs, old buddy. And we go back and get the first machine . . . wherever the hell it is."

That thought brought him up short for a moment. Certainly, that first machine had to be somewhere. Only *where?* It should have merely traveled back into the past ten minutes, from the time he'd sent it off, right in that very selfsame lab, and only been gone for ten seconds. Only, of course, since the auto-return module had switched itself off, it hadn't returned ten seconds later and was undoubtedly still there. Which meant he had to work out the precise settings so that he would go back into the past exactly ten minutes from the time he had originally sent the first machine back. Or did he?

If it was still in the lab, and time was sort of linear, and the new past he had altered by sending back the machine was running about ten minutes behind him, then it was probably still there, only ten minutes ago.

Unless I've moved it, he thought. Only why would I do that? If I sent it back and the past me saw it appear, and not return, then obviously the past me in that new, altered linear past would have figured out that something had gone wrong and would undoubtedly be waiting for the future me to figure it all out.

"Is that what I'd do?" he asked himself aloud. "Well, yes, of course, since I thought of it, then that's exactly what I'd do, since I'm me and I know how I think, whether I'm the present me or the past me. Right?" He glanced at Bugs and nodded. "Right. Of course. That makes sense, doesn't it?"

Bugs merely continued munching on his lettuce leaf.

"The past me must be getting very impatient with the present me, or from the past me's viewpoint, the *future* me, to figure it all out and fix it. And all this time, it was so obvious. When I get back there, I'll have to give myself a good talking to."

The thing to do, he decided, was duplicate the original settings exactly, without attempting to compensate for the time lag from the date of the original experiment. Just repeat everything exactly the same way and travel back into the past ten minutes earlier from the present. That way, the first time machine would undoubtedly still be there, and he would be too, since he'd arrived at the lab considerably more than ten minutes ago.

He frowned and scratched his head. He hadn't seen himself when he came in, so clearly, that seemed to support his new theory that time ran in a sort of linear fashion, rather like the current of a river. He tried to visualize it.

If he were sitting on a riverbank and he marked a certain place on that bank with a stone, then took a flower petal, for instance, and dropped it in the river some distance upstream of the stone, then he could watch the flower petal as it drifted downstream, past the stone. That was the normal flow of time. A few seconds in the past, the flower petal had been *upstream* of the stone, now it was *downstream* of it.

If he now fished that flower petal out of the water, carried it back to the spot where he'd originally dropped it in, and went back a moment or so in the past and dropped it in again, there would now be *two* flower petals floating downstream, side by side, toward the stone. However, since there had to be a space of time in which there had only been *one* flower petal floating down the river, that space of time was now represented by the volume of water from which he had fished out the flower petal before taking it back upstream and traveling back into the past with it.

Consequently, the two flower petals now floating downstream side by side would be aware of each other (assuming awareness on the part of flower petals), but the flower petal in the original, unaltered space of time represented by the volume of water between the place where he had originally tossed it in the river and the place where he had fished it out would have no awareness of a second flower petal, because in that particular time frame, its past had not been changed. The past had been changed *behind* it.

Brewster figured this was why he was unaware of having seen himself when he walked into the laboratory a short while ago. Because he was still existing in that space of time where the past had not yet been changed. The moment he went back, he'd see himself entering the lab, but he couldn't remember that now because it hadn't happened yet. It had happened—or *would* happen—about ten minutes earlier.

He looked at the rabbit. "I sure wish you could talk, Bugs," he said. "It would help clear up a lot of things."

He entered the settings into the console on the panel, programming his trip, and wondered what it would feel like to meet himself. About ten minutes ago, he'd find out.

He took a deep breath, wondering why he didn't feel a sense of incredible elation. He was, after all, about to become the first man in history to travel back through time. Even if it was only ten minutes. The elation, he supposed, would probably come later, when he published his discovery and EnGulfCo got behind him with its massive public relations machine.

There would be lectures at universities, interviews in magazines and newspapers, appearances on talk shows, perhaps even a film about his life, all culminating, certainly, in the awarding of the Nobel Prize. Doubtless, that would bring it all home to him and he would feel elated then. Right now, all he felt was a slight tension, an anxiety that always came just before an important project was successfully completed.

He thought of Pamela. She would be so proud of him. This would make up for his having missed all those wedding dates. After this, they could finally get married and then he could take her on a wonderful honeymoon. Perhaps to Victorian London, he thought, or to Paris during the reign of the Sun King.

"Well, Bugs, here goes," he said, and flipped the switch.

CHAPTER
T W O

Michael Timothy O'Fallon was, on the whole, having a very pleasant afternoon. The sun was bright, the sky was clear, his pipe was full, and he had absolutely nothing to do. He had filled all his orders, and for once, there were no annoying customers to deal with. He often wished there was some way he could conduct his business without having to deal with the public, but unfortunately, he had not yet found a way around this necessary evil. In order to sell the fruits of his labors, he required customers to buy them and Mick O'Fallon regarded customers as an irritating inconvenience. They were always pestering him, always haggling, always impatient, and always trying to look over his shoulder as he worked—which was not very difficult to do, as Mick was only three feet tall.

He was, however, almost equally as wide, with an immensely powerful upper body and short, muscular legs, which often led people to mistake him for a dwarf, something that infuriated him no end. As far as he was concerned dwarfs were obnoxious little cretins who dressed in loud and clashing colors, had little intelligence to speak of, and were only good for relatively undemanding, menial labor. The finer aspects of any sort of real craft were utterly beyond them, though they were industrious, Mick had to give them that. Give them some simple, mindless physical task to perform and they'd happily pitch in, singing and whistling while they worked. Nevertheless, being mistaken for a dwarf was rather insulting, especially if one happened to be a leprechaun.

Mick was not especially sanguine on this issue. Whenever some customer made this mistake, Mick would start to turn crimson, all his facial muscles would get tight, and using all his self-control in an effort to keep his temper, he would pointedly and firmly correct them in no uncertain terms. Then he would go out behind his shop, snarling and trembling with fury all the way, clamp his massive arms around the trunk of some tree, and, with one mighty heave, uproot it. In this way, he had systematically cleared a large section of the woods around his shop.

However, on this bright and sunny day, there were no customers around to irritate him and he had fulfilled all his commissions, so he had packed his tobacco pouch and pipe and hiked up the trail to the top of Lookout Mountain, to simply bask in the sun and smoke and laze away the day while he enjoyed the view. It wasn't an especially tall mountain, but it *was* an especially nice view.

He was enjoying the peace and quiet and the solitude when the air above him suddenly became filled with static discharges and an extremely loud and high-pitched whining sound. He glanced up and saw a very strange-looking contraption suddenly appear out of nowhere in the sky about twenty feet above him, to an accompanying clap of thunder, and proceed to fall at an alarming rate directly toward the spot where he was sitting.

With a yelp, he threw himself out of the way, just in the

nick of time, as the mysterious object struck the ground with a jarring crash, barely missing him, and proceeded to slide down the grassy mountain slope on what looked like sled runners, picking up speed as it went. It plowed through bushes and jounced over rocks protruding from the mountain slope, sending off sparks as it careened precariously down toward the bottom. Mick wasn't sure, but for a moment, it seemed as if he'd heard a voice issuing from inside the peculiar-looking object, crying, *"Helllllp!"*

"The devil!" Mick exclaimed as he dusted himself off and watched the thing go crashing down the mountainside, going faster and faster, slipping sideways and tipping from one runner to the other, miraculously without overbalancing, kept more or less right side up by some kind of large and shiny ring that encircled it diagonally.

"Faith, and I've never seen the like of it!" he said, watching thunderstruck as the strange object hurtled down the mountain slope until it finally came to a crashing halt against the trunk of a huge tree. The object struck the tree with a resounding impact, shooting sparks all over the place. The tree shuddered, cracked, then splintered and, with a loud and agonizingly drawn-out creaking sound, came crashing down onto the ground, narrowly missing Robie McMurphy's prize bull, which had been grazing peacefully at the edge of the wood.

"Oh, dear," said Mick. He picked up his pipe and hurried down the trail as quickly as his short, muscular legs could carry him.

Brewster was stunned by the impact and he blacked out for a short while, but fortunately, his seat belt and his air bag safety system had prevented any serious injury. Nevertheless, Brewster was badly shaken up. Dazed, he tried to focus his vision and figure out what had happened, but everything seemed to be shrouded in a thick, white mist. (In fact, his face was enveloped in the air bag, but he hadn't quite figured that out yet.)

His head was throbbing, he felt dizzy, and his entire body ached. With a high-pitched, whiny-squeaky sound, not unlike that of air escaping from a set of bagpipes, the air bag slowly deflated and Brewster gratefully gulped in a deep lungful of air. Then he heard a dull *clunk*, followed by a soft *whump*, as the emergency parachute was automatically deployed—a trifle late. It settled down over the cracked and shattered cockpit, obscuring everything from view.

For a moment all was still, save for the crackling and sparking of the ruined control panel and electrical systems, then the entire framework of the time machine rocked as something struck it a tremendous blow. Brewster was thrown sideways in his seat, but the belt restrained him as the machine shuddered under the impact. He heard a loud *crack* as something gave way and the entire cockpit became filled with sparks.

There was a loud, angry, bellowing sound, followed by the sound of galloping hoofbeats, and then the machine shuddered once again as Robie McMurphy's enraged bull plowed into it, head down, with the speed of an express train. Of course, Brewster didn't know exactly what was happening. He was still dazed and stunned, and he couldn't see anything because of the red and white striped parachute draped over the cockpit. However, in the dim recesses of his mind, perhaps prompted by the instinct for self-preservation, a thought managed to form itself and squirm through the haze that enshrouded his consciousness.

"The LOX!"

As Robie McMurphy's bull smashed into the time machine once again, Brewster realized that with all these sparks, if the liquid oxygen tanks ruptured, there was liable to be a very big bang, indeed. Panic and adrenaline coursed through him as he fumbled with his seat belt. The bull attacked the offending machine yet again and Brewster was almost thrown out of his seat.

"Oh, God," he said, "the LOX! The LOX!"

He shielded his eyes against a fresh burst of sparks from the arcing control panel.

"Hallo!" a strange voice called out. "I say, is someone in there?"

"Get me out of here!" Brewster shouted, desperately trying to force open the damaged door of the cockpit. "The LOX! The LOX!"

Mick frowned. Locks? he thought. Faith, the poor chap must be locked up in there. He couldn't get out. He started tugging on the parachute, trying to pull it free. The contraption was sputtering and sparking and there was a strange smell in the air around it. He sidestepped quickly as the bull made another maddened charge and slammed into the peculiar-looking object, sending forth a fresh shower of sparks as it bellowed with rage.

"Bugger off, you great big stupid thing, you!" Mick yelled at it. He resumed tugging at the parachute as the bull backed off for another go.

Brewster saw daylight as the chute was pulled away. He also saw flames start licking from the control panel and started kicking at the door with all his might. It wouldn't budge.

"Hold on now, I'll have you out in a flash!" the voice called, and then, with the sound of ripping metal and cracking plastic, the door was torn right off the cockpit hinges. Brewster made a dive for the opening.

"Quickly, quickly!" he said as he scrambled out, dragging his emergency supply kit with him. "We've got to get away! The LOX..." and then he saw the charging bull, bearing straight down at him. *"Jesus!"*

He was suddenly swept off his feet and thrown over a shoulder (a very *low* shoulder, it seemed) and he gasped with surprise as his rescuer started running with him as if he didn't weigh a thing. Behind them, the bull smashed into the time machine for the final time. It was the final time because, just as Brewster had feared, the liquid oxygen tanks ruptured and the mixture ignited. The resulting explosion hurled them both to the ground, where bits of machinery and very well-cooked beefsteak rained down on them.

Brewster covered his head and lay there on the ground, the wind knocked out of him. For what seemed like a long time, he didn't move. And then he heard a voice say, *"Great bloody leaping toadstools!* What the devil was *that?"*

It was the voice of his unknown benefactor, whom Brewster hadn't even caught a clear glimpse of yet. He raised himself up slightly and turned his head, then his eyes grew wide at the sight of his rescuer. He did a double take.

At first glance, it looked like a small boy, albeit a rather large and powerfully built small boy, but at second glance, he realized it was a full-grown man. Well, perhaps "full grown" was not quite the proper term, but an adult, at any rate, with a bushy beard, shaggy brown hair that was beginning to turn gray, and a chest and arms like a bodybuilder— on a miniature scale.

A dwarf, he thought (and it was probably fortunate that he only *thought* this rather than saying it out loud), then he mentally corrected himself when he saw that the man, while very small, was nevertheless perfectly proportioned, which made him not a dwarf, but a midget. A little person,

Brewster mentally corrected himself again. They don't like to be called midgets, they like to be called little people.

"*My bull!*" a new voice suddenly cried out. "*What have you done to my prize bull?*"

A man was running toward them across the field, shaking his fist and, in his other hand, brandishing a very nasty-looking pitchfork. He was dressed in a peculiar fashion, tight black breeches and what appeared to be a brown potato sack belted around his waist, with a hole in it for his head and arms. He was wearing high, soft leather moccasins and he had long, shoulder-length hair. For that matter, the little man who'd rescued him was dressed in a peculiar fashion too, thought Brewster. He had on some kind of belted, brown leather jerkin cut in scallops around the hem and sleeves, baggy green trousers tucked into high, laced leather boots, and a large dagger at his waist. Brewster wondered if he hadn't somehow transported himself to some sort of hippie commune in the country. Or perhaps these were circus people. In fact, he wondered, where *had* he transported himself? He should have been back in the lab, but this most definitely was not his laboratory. He glanced around. It wasn't even London. Something had very definitely gone wrong.

"Mick O'Fallon!" said the farmer as he came running up. "I should have known you'd be at the bottom of this! You and your blasted alchemical mixtures! Now look what you've gone and done! You've killed my bull!"

"S'trewth, and I didn't touch your bleedin' bull, Robie McMurphy," the little man said as he got up to a sitting position. "And have a care, or can you not recognize a wizard when you see one?"

The farmer's eyes grew wide as he gazed at Brewster. "A wizard!" he exclaimed.

"A master sorcerer, I should think," said Mick, "judgin'

by the way he blasted that great, big, foolish bull of yours. You'd best show proper respect, else you're liable to find yourself gettin' some of the same."

"Beggin' your pardon, Good Master," said McMurphy, lowering his gaze and dropping to one knee. "I didn't know!"

"Dropped right out of the sky, he did," said Mick, "in some kind of magic chariot. Faith, and didn't I see it myself?"

Brewster blinked at them with confusion. "Where am I?" he asked, looking around him. The countryside didn't look familiar, but then again, he hadn't spent much time outside of London. Then his gaze fell on the blasted, smoldering wreckage of his time machine. "Oh, no! Ruined! It's absolutely ruined!"

"Your stupid, bloody bull attacked his magic chariot," Mick said to the farmer, by way of explanation.

McMurphy looked chagrined. More than that, he suddenly looked terrified. "Forgive me, Good Master!" he pleaded. "I beg of you, don't punish me! I shall make amends, somehow, I swear it!"

Brewster wasn't paying very close attention. Now that the fireworks were over, it was dawning on him that he must have seriously miscalculated. Somehow, he had transported himself right out of the city and, worse still, the machine had been utterly destroyed. Now he would have to find out exactly where he was and call Pamela to come and pick him up. He sighed heavily. She was bound to be very much annoyed. He'd have to ask these people if he could use a telephone.

Then it suddenly occurred to him that he hadn't even thanked the little man for pulling him out of the time machine before it exploded and thereby saving his life. He turned back toward him, somewhat sheepishly.

"I'm sorry," he said to the little man, "I'm forgetting my manners. I'm very grateful for your help. The door was stuck and if you hadn't forced it open . . ." He swallowed nervously as he considered his narrow escape. "Allow me to introduce myself. The name is Brewster. Dr. Marvin Brewster. But my friends just call me Doc." He held out his hand.

The little man reached out and clasped him by the forearm, rather than the hand. Brewster assumed this was some sort of new counterculture handshake and he politely did the same.

"Honored to be makin' your acquaintance, Brewster Doc," the little man said. "As it happens, I do a bit of brewin' on the side myself, y'know. Of course, I'm strictly a layman, a dabbler, as it were. I am a craftsman, by trade, an armorer."

"You don't say," said Brewster absently. "Listen, do you mind if I use your phone? I'll make it collect, but I need to call London."

The little man frowned. "Fone?" he said quizzically. He shook his head. "Faith, and I have no such thing, I fear. And I know of no Lunden hereabouts."

Now it was Brewster's turn to frown. "You don't know London?"

"I know of no one by that name, Good Brewster," Mick replied.

"No, no, I mean the city," Brewster said. "London, the city."

The little man and the farmer exchanged puzzled glances. "I know of no such city," said Mick. "Is it very far?"

"I don't know," Brewster replied. "I'm not quite sure where I am, you see. I seem to have miscalculated, somehow. What is this place?"

"My farm," McMurphy said, trying to be helpful.

"No, no, I mean what *town*?" said Brewster.

" '*Town*'?" McMurphy said. He looked around, uncertainly. "But . . . there is no town here, Good Master. The nearest village would be Brigand's Roost, I suppose."

"Brigand's Roost?" Brewster frowned again. He had never even heard of it.

"Well," said McMurphy, "until the brigands came, it used to be called Turkey's Roost, but the brigands shot most of the turkeys and ate them."

Brewster was having some difficulty following the conversation. " '*Brigands*'? What do you mean, 'brigands'?"

"He means Black Shannon's brigands," Mick said. "They used to live in the forest, and then they were called the Forest Brigands, only Shannon decided the forest lacked certain amenities, so they took over Turkey's Roost, which is now called Brigand's Roost, you see."

Brewster didn't see at all. "What, you mean they actually took over a town?"

"Only a small village, really," said Mick, "and not much of one, at that."

"What are they, some sort of motorcycle gang?" asked Brewster.

McMurphy and Mick both looked blank. Clearly, they had no idea what he was talking about.

Brewster began to have an unsettling feeling about all this. They didn't know about London, they didn't seem to have telephones or know what motorcycles were, they had brigands, and the clothing they were wearing was either very hip or very out-of-date.

"What . . . *year* is this?" asked Brewster.

They both looked blank again. They exchanged puzzled glances. McMurphy looked at Mick and shrugged. Mick shook his head.

"Forgive me, Brewster," Mick said, "I don't understand."

"Oh, boy," said Brewster.

Mick stiffened and drew himself up to his full height, all three feet of it. "I am no boy, Brewster," he said with affronted dignity. "I am one of the little people."

"What?" said Brewster. "Oh. No, I'm sorry, you misunderstood. I know you are a little person, I was merely saying 'Oh, boy' as an expression."

"An expression of what?" asked Mick.

"Dismay, I think," Brewster replied.

The full import of what had happened to him was only beginning to register. (It would take a while yet, but let's bring him along slowly, shall we? He's a nice enough fella, even if he doesn't have a lot of street smarts, and we don't want to give it to him all at once.) Now let me think, he thought, and proceeded to do just that.

He had set the machine to take him back ten minutes into the past, at the exact same location from which he had departed. Obviously, this was *not* the exact same location from which he had departed, so it stood to reason that it probably wasn't ten minutes in the past, either.

The reason he had crashed, he deduced, was that he had been located on the top floor of the headquarters building of EnGulfCo International when he had left. He had arrived at some point in space and time where that building did not exist. Ergo, he'd had a bit of a drop. Fortunately, he happened to arrive over a mountain, otherwise, the drop would have been a great deal more significant. Fortunately, also, that the steel torus had kept the machine from tumbling, otherwise the tanks might have ruptured on the way down the mountain slope and the results would have been fatal. And it was fortunate that the little man named Mick had been there to force the door loose, but right about there, the few fortunate things about this entire episode ended.

He had clearly traveled a lot further back into the past than he'd intended. He wasn't quite sure how. In the initial experiments he had conducted with Bugs, everything seemed to have worked perfectly. But then, for all he knew, Bugs had *also* traveled back further into the past than he'd thought. The encouraging thing was that Bugs had made it back, and in one piece. The discouraging thing was that unlike Bugs, Brewster no longer had a ride. Unless . . .

There was still that first time machine, the one that had departed on a one-way trip, thanks to the faulty switch in the auto-return module. The settings on both machines had been the same. Therefore, it stood to reason that the first machine was here, as well. Wherever "here" was. At least, Brewster earnestly hoped that was the case; otherwise, he was stuck.

Brewster approached the still-smoking wreckage of what used to be his time machine and stared at it disconsolately.

"I am truly sorry about your chariot, Good Brewster," said McMurphy uneasily. "If there is any way that I can make amends, you have but to ask and I shall do it, if 'tis within my power."

"Hmmm," said Brewster. "Perhaps there is. You wouldn't happen to have seen another, uh, chariot like that around here anywhere, would you?"

McMurphy frowned. "I do not think so, Good Master. What did it look like?"

"Oh, yes, of course, you didn't really see it, did you?" Brewster said. He turned to Mick. "*You* got a good look at it, though, didn't you? Would you recognize one that was just like it if you saw it?"

"Aye, that I would," said Mick confidently.

"So then you've seen one before?" asked Brewster eagerly.

"I can say with certitude that I have not," Mick replied.

"Oh," said Brewster, his spirits falling. He sighed. *Now* what?

* * *

"Well, 'tis not much, but 'tis home," said Mick as Brewster ducked down low to get through the tiny doorway. "Bit close for someone your size," added Mick apologetically, "but I don't get much company, you see."

"Oh, it's . . . charming," said Brewster, bent over almost completely double to avoid banging his head on the ceiling.

The little thatch-roofed cabin in the woods looked like a child's playhouse, set in a clearing next to a somewhat larger structure made of stone that housed Mick's forge and shop.

"You'd likely be more comfortable in the smithy," Mick said, "but I'll have to clean it up some. Still, at least there's room for a human to stretch out in there."

"You're very kind," said Brewster. "I really appreciate your hospitality. I wouldn't want to put you to any trouble."

"Oh, 'tis no trouble at all, Good Brewster," Mick replied. " 'Tis not every day I have the privilege to entertain a great personage such as yourself."

"I wish you'd call me Doc," said Brewster. "All my friends call me Doc."

"Well, 'tis a privilege, indeed," said Mick. "Doc it shall be, then. My full name is Michael Timothy O'Fallon, at your service, but most people call me Mick. Are you a drinkin' man?"

"Yes, I think I could use a drink," said Brewster, sitting down cross-legged behind a large, albeit very low, table.

"I have just the thing," said Mick, producing a pair of tankards, which he filled from a large ceramic jug. Brewster noticed that although most things in the little cabin were on a miniature scale, the tankards were certainly man-sized.

Mick raised his tankard solemnly and offered a toast. "May your path be free of dragons, and may your life be long. May you never lack for maidens that will fill your heart with song. May your courage never waver and your blade be ever true, and should your enemy be braver, may he not run as fast as you."

He looked at Brewster expectantly.

"Uh . . . over the lips and past the gums, look out, stomach, here it comes," Brewster said rather lamely.

Mick beamed and drained his tankard at one gulp, then smacked his lips, patted his middle, and said, "Ahhhhh."

Brewster took a sip and gagged. It felt as if he'd swallowed drain cleaner. The noxious liquid burned its way down his esophagus like sulphuric acid spiked with white phosphorus. His eyes bugged out and he made a sound like the death rattle of a horse as he clutched at his throat and fought for breath.

"Good, eh?" Mick said, grinning at him. " 'Tis my special recipie. Brewed from the root of the peregrine bush. 'Tis a lengthy process, unless you don't count the time it takes to chase down the damn bushes and wrestle 'em to the ground. Thorny little bastards, too."

Brewster was turning an interesting shade of mottled purple.

"Of course, 'tis the agin' process that makes all the difference," Mick continued, refilling his own tankard. He held the jug up and raised his eyebrows, but all Brewster could manage was a violent shake of his head and an emphysemic wheeze.

"So then," Mick continued, taking another hearty swallow of the odious brew, "if I understand correctly, your chariot has brought you here from a distant city known as London, but there was somethin' to the spell that went amiss, as this was not the intended destination of your journey, am I right, then?"

Brewster gasped for breath and nodded weakly. His vision was starting to blur.

" 'Tis the sort of thing that happens, sometimes, with a spell," said Mick, nodding sympathetically. "Even to the best of wizards. It's happened to me, y'know, with some of my potions, not that I claim to be an adept, of course. Far be it from me to do any such foolish thing. I know the law, I do. I'm merely a student of the art of alchemy. 'Tis a hobby, bein' as I'm one of the little people and therefore fey, though 'tis a shame we're not permitted to join the Guild."

While Mick loquaciously warmed to his subject, Brewster simply sat there with his eyes glazing over. He didn't really hear what Mick was saying because of the loud buzzing in his ears.

"Not that I'm complainin', mind you," Mick continued. "I'm sure the directors of the Guild know best, and I would never gainsay them, but I do think we little people have somethin' to contribute. 'Tisn't true, y'know, that we're all mischievous and devious tricksters. I've no idea how that rumor got about, for there's not a grain of truth to it. Still, there you have it."

Brewster's pupils had become extremely dilated. He couldn't move a muscle.

"My customers come to me because they know my reputation as a craftsman," Mick went on. "You'll not find a better blade in these parts than one forged by Mick O'Fallon, mind you, yet each and every one of them comes thinkin' that I'll cheat them. 'Tis what they've been brought up to expect from leprechauns, y'see. Malicious gossip. Not a word of truth in it. Don't ask me how it all got started, I haven't the faintest clue. Unless it was the elves. I wouldn't put it past them. Never did trust elves. Bloody great lot of troublemakers, if you ask me. Never did a lick of honest work in their lives. Spend all their time sittin' 'round in coffeehouses, playin' their guitars and talkin' about philosophy and whatnot. Ever try to have a conversation with an elf? 'Tis like openin' a book in the bloody middle.''

Without a word, Brewster slowly keeled over and crashed to the floor.

"Oh, dear," said Mick, staring at his inert form on the floor. "Poor chap must've been tired from his journey, and here I am, talkin' his ear off. Well, we'll make up a nice straw bed for you in the smithy and let you have a nice rest, shall we? Then in the mornin', perhaps if you're not too busy, you might take a look at my alchemical laboratory."

He got up from his chair, went around the table, and effortlessly picked Brewster up in his arms. He was as stiff as a dead carp.

"Never had the benefit of a real sorcerer's advice, y'know," said Mick. "Always had to muddle through sort of on me own. Still, if you're stuck here till you can build another magic chariot, well then, perhaps you might consider takin' me on as an apprentice. I'm a good worker, I am. Learn fast, too. Never can tell, if I get good enough, I might even convince the Guild to let me join, though of course, that's probably too much to hope for."

He smacked Brewster's head against the door frame as he carried him out of the house to the smithy.

"Ooops. Sorry about that. Feelin' no pain, are you? Good. Be a bit of a bump though. Tell him he got it when he fell over. Aye, that's what I'll do."

He carried Brewster into the smithy and prepared a straw bed, well away from the forge, just to be on the safe side. Then he laid him down gently and covered him with a frayed and faded blanket.

"There, I guess that'll do you proper. Sleep well, Brewster Doc. In the mornin' we'll see about gettin' you settled. We haven't had a sorcerer in these parts for quite a spell, no pun intended. Folks will be right pleased and excited. Never know, you might even consider stayin'. I imagine there's many adepts in a big city like your London. What's one less, eh? Sure, and they'll never miss you."

Brewster awoke in the morning to something rubbing up against him. It felt scratchy. He grunted and rolled over onto his other side. He frowned. His bed felt funny. He had always liked a hard mattress, but the bed felt very soft for some strange reason and it crackled when he moved. It also felt somewhat bristly. He frowned and lay still for a moment, still on the edge of wakefulness. Something rubbed up against him once again and he felt a pricking sensation.

"Ouch! Pamela, stop that," he mumbled. "Your nails are long."

He shifted in bed and once again felt it crackle beneath him. It also smelled strange, he suddenly noticed. He sniffed several times experimentally. The scent was not unpleasant. He opened his eyes and found that he was lying on a bed of straw.

Straw? For a moment he felt disoriented. And then something started rubbing up against him once again, with a rustling sort of sound, and he felt that same scratchy, prickling sensation.

"Pamela . . ."

He rolled over and got a faceful of leaves and sharp little thorns. He cried out with pain and surprise, recoiled, and rolled out of the straw bed onto the floor. With a convulsive, rustling movement, the small bush recoiled in the opposite direction, scuttling off toward the wall, where it seemed to huddle fearfully, it's reddish-gold, heart-shaped leaves trembling slightly.

"What the hell . . ." said Brewster, staring at the little bush, wide-eyed.

Tentatively, the little bush scuttled forward, moving toward him a few feet. Brewster backed away, crablike, across the floor. The little bush stopped, its leaves rustling. Then it started moving toward him once again.

Alarmed, Brewster scooted back against the opposite wall. "Get back!" he cried out.

The little bush scuttled backward a few feet, its leaves trembling once again.

"Ah, so you're up then," Mick said. He picked up a straw broom from the corner and urged the little bush away. "Go on now, off with you! Go on, get! Stop annoying the company, you foolish thing, you!"

Bewildered, Brewster watched as the little red-gold bush retreated from the broom wielded by the little man. "What *is* it?" he asked, astonished.

"What, this useless thing?" Mick jerked his head toward the bush, now cowering uncertainly in a corner, its leaves trembling violently. "Why, 'tis a peregrine bush, Doc."

"A peregrine bush?"

"Aye, you'll recall I was tellin' you last night how y'have to chase the damn things down to make the brew? Peregrine wine, I call it."

The bush started to tremble even more violently.

"Oh, calm down, you silly thing," Mick snapped at it. "I'm not for cookin' you up yet, though if you don't behave yourself, I just might toss you in the pot for good measure." He turned to Brewster. "Wouldn't do much good, really. This one's still too immature. Make the wine taste bitter and it wouldn't be nearly so potent, y'see."

Brewster rubbed his head. "It seemed pretty potent last night," he said, though strangely, he didn't have anything resembling a hangover. Only a slight bump on his head he must have got from falling over. Just the same, that one swallow had been enough to paralyze him.

"Ah, well, it takes some gettin' used to," Mick explained.

"I've never heard of a bush that could move," said Brewster, "except for tumbleweeds, and they're blown by the wind."

"Are they, now?" said Mick. "Well, I've never heard of these tumbleweeds myself, but there's more peregrine bushes than you can shake a stick at in these parts. Most of the time, they just stay planted in the soil, as any decent, self-respectin' shrub should do, but sometimes they just uproot themselves and take to wanderin' about. Every year around this time, they pull up their roots and start travelin' like a great big thorny herd, from Birnam Wood all the way to Dunsinane Hill. Faith, and I don't know why. They just do, that's all. Birnam to Dunsinane, Dunsinane to Birnam, back and forth, like a bloody, great ambulatory hedge. Like enough to drive you mad, and there's no turnin' 'em. You get yourself caught in their path and you're liable to get sliced to ribbons."

"That's incredible," said Brewster. "I've never heard of such a thing! Migratory *bushes*?"

"Aye, silly, isn't it? But there you have it. This one's just a wee sprout. I keep it about to amuse me, and so's I can learn a bit about their habits, the better to catch 'em when their roots are ripe, y'see. But it's a bloody stupid thing. Harmless, really, but always gettin' underfoot. Still, it kind of grows on you. Grows on you! That's a good one, eh? Grows on you!" Mick cackled and slapped his muscular thigh.

Brewster eyed the little thorn bush apprehensively. Its leaves seemed to be drooping dejectedly.

"I don't seem to remember very much about last night," he said. "Did you bring me here?"

"Aye, that I did, after you passed out. Never did see it hit anyone quite so hard before, but I suppose if you're not used to it, the wine can have a bit of a kick."

"I'll say," said Brewster.

"You'll say what?" asked Mick.

"That it can have a bit of a kick," said Brewster. "Strange, though, I feel particularly refreshed this morning."

"It has that effect on you," Mick replied, nodding. "You have to be careful, though. Drink enough of the stuff and you'll want to be takin' on an army all by yourself. The brigands buy it from me by the cartload, they do. Use up just about every batch I brew each year. Drink so much of it, they're all a bit touched in the head." Mick tapped his cranium for emphasis.

"Brigands," Brewster repeated. "Brigands and migratory bushes. What sort of place *is* this? Where am I, exactly, Mick?"

"S'trewth, and this London of yours must be terribly far off. Well, to be exact now, you're in Mick O'Fallon's smithy, next to Mick O'Fallon's cottage at the edge of the Redwood Forest, by the Gulfstream Waters."

"That sounds vaguely familiar, for some reason," Brewster said, frowning, "though I can't for the life of me remember why." Without realizing it, he hummed half a bar of "This Land Is Your Land." He shook his head and shrugged. "Can't place it. We are still in England, though, right?"

"Ing Land?" Mick said, frowning. "Faith, Doc, 'tis not Ing Land. S'trewth, and I've never heard of this Ing Land. You are in the Kingdom of Frank."

"The Kingdom of *Frank*?" said Brewster.

"Aye, the Kingdom of Frank. It used to be the Kingdom of Corwin, y'see, only Frank the Usurper had him murdered and then usurped the throne, bein' as that's what usurpers do. He issued a decree that had the name changed to the Kingdom of Frank. 'Twas a long time ago, and all the kings since then have been named Frank, y'see, because 'tis easier than changin' the name of the kingdom every time a new heir to the throne comes along.''

Brewster looked as if he wasn't sure if Mick was pulling his leg or not. "Are you pulling my leg?" he asked.

"Well, now why would I want to do a thing like that?" asked Mick, puzzled.

"We are in the Kingdom of *Frank*?"

"Aye, the Kingdom of Frank, in the Land of Darn."

" 'Darn'?" said Brewster, looking totally confused.

"You mean to tell me you've never heard of Darn?" said Mick with surprise. "Faith, and y'must have come a fair long way, then. Aye, I suppose you must have, for I have never heard of Ing Land, neither."

"Where *is* Darn?" Brewster asked.

"Why, on the edge of the Gulfstream Waters, of course," Mick said. "Tis named for Darn the Navigator, who first discovered it, y'see."

"Darn the Navigator?" Brewster said, staring at Mick blankly.

"Aye. He discovered it by mistake. He was lost, y'see."

Brewster closed his eyes. "This isn't really happening," he said. "I'm just having a dream. None of this is real. I'm going to wake up any minute now and Pamela will be lying right beside me, wearing her green face mask."

"You sleep with a wench that wears a mask?" said Mick. "S'trewth, and if she was that ugly, why did you take up with her? Or is it that she came with a grand dowry?"

"Nope," said Brewster, shaking his head. "Nope, this isn't happening." He glanced toward the corner. "Come here, bush."

The bush rustled slightly.

"Come on, I won't hurt you," Brewster cajoled. "Come over here."

Hesitantly, the bush rustled over toward him. Brewster reached out and stuck his hand into its thorny branches.

"OW!"

The bush rapidly retreated to its corner, where it huddled, quaking.

"Well, now what did you want to go and do a thing like that for?" Mick asked, frowning at him.

Brewster stared at the scratches on his hand. They weren't very deep, because the bush was small and its thorns weren't very long, but it had hurt just the same. He watched as thin lines of blood welled up in the cuts.

"I'm not dreaming," he said in a dazed tone, "unless I'm dreaming *this*, too." He tried to recall if he'd ever dreamed of feeling pain.

Mick came over and stood before him, staring at him with concern. "Sure, and it's no dream you're havin', Doc," he said. "I can see you're troubled, what with your magic chariot bein' broke and all, but in time, you can build yourself another. In the meantime, 'tis not as if you're all alone, y'know. You've got Mick O'Fallon to stand by you."

Brewster sighed. "You don't understand, Mick," he said morosely. "It's not that easy. You've been very kind, and I appreciate your hospitality, but my, uh, magic chariot is beyond repair, and I doubt I'll ever be able to build another one. I'll simply never be able to find the necessary materials here. The conditions seem much too primitive. I'm afraid I've traveled a great deal further than I intended. And there may be no way back."

"Well, the journey may be long," said Mick, "yet each journey begins with but a single step, y'know. In due time, after you've rested and we've made some plans, you can make your way to the coast and find a ship that'll take you across the Gulfstream Waters, back to your London, in the Land of Ing."

"I'm afraid it's not that simple, Mick," said Brewster. "Where I need to go, no ship can take me, unless it's a ship that can travel across time."

Mick frowned, puzzled. "I don't understand," he said.

Brewster took a deep breath. "Well, it'll take some explaining," he said. "And, quite frankly, I don't think you'll believe me. It's a long story."

"Is it now?" said Mick with a smile. "Well, it just so happens that I'm in the mood for a good story. Come on, then. You can tell me all about it over breakfast."

CHAPTER
T H R E E

Brewster had never been in the habit of having much more for breakfast than a cup of coffee and a piece of toast or two. Yet, despite the fact that he was rather hungry for a change, Brewster knew he could never even make a dent in all the provender that Mick had laid out on the table. He now knew where the phrase "groaning board" had come from.

"There, now, I think that should do for a wee mornin' snack," said Mick, surveying the table with pleasure and smacking his lips over the smoked meats, the huge circular bread loaves, the jars of preserves and jams and jellies, the basket of hard-boiled eggs, the sausages, the vegetables, the roast turkey, the fruits, the flapjacks, the pot of tea, and of course, the jug of peregrine wine.

"Dig in, Doc, before your belly starts a-rumblin'."

Brewster watched, astonished, as his host tore off a large turkey leg and devoured it in less time than it took him to put honey in his tea.

Breakfast with a leprechaun can be a rather disquieting experience if you're not used to it, as only dwarfs and

43

dragons are known to have greater appetites. Dwarfs, however, are slightly larger in stature than most leprechauns, and dragons are considerably larger, but Brewster didn't know about either dwarfs or dragons yet. In fact, he didn't even know about leprechauns, exactly, because he still hadn't fully realized what sort of situation his time machine had popped him into and he thought Mick was a midget.

To be perfectly fair, Brewster's ignorance up to this point was not entirely inexcusable. While Mick had made a point of mentioning that he was one of the "little people," the term also happened to apply to midgets in the world that Brewster came from, so Brewster had not connected it with leprechauns. Perhaps he might have noticed that Mick's ears were unusually large and slightly pointed (unlike elves, whose ears are in proportion, but are very pointed), only Mick wore his hair rather long and shaggy and Brewster never really got a good look at his ears. And the previous night, while Mick had been discussing things like elves and such, Brewster had not been in any condition to pay very close attention.

Now, the peregrine bush did, indeed, come as a bit of a surprise to him, and you might think that would have clued him in to the fact that he wasn't in Kansas anymore, as a little girl named Dorothy once put it. However, if there's one thing scientists know, especially the very bright ones, it's that there is an awful lot they *don't* know. This is why they're scientists.

Botany was never Brewster's field of expertise. Though he had never heard of migratory bushes, he knew that didn't necessarily mean such things did not exist. Quite obviously, they *did* exist, for he had seen one. And been scratched by one, no less. Had Brewster been a botanist, he would have known there was no record of any such plant as a peregrine bush. However, in that case, rather than immediately leaping to the conclusion that he had somehow been transported to another world, chances were he would have thought he'd made a new discovery. He would undoubtedly have become tremendously excited, with visions of publication and Latin names such as *Philodendron Brewstoricus* dancing through his head. But Brewster was not a botanist, and as is often the case with scientists, he was not terribly concerned with any new developments outside his chosen field. He found the peregrine bush merely a peculiar curiosity and nothing more.

For the moment he had a rather more pressing problem on his hands. Namely, trying to figure out where the hell in space and time he was. This is how scientists are, you understand. When they're working on a knotty problem, they tend not to let little distractions like ambulatory bushes get in their way.

History was not Brewster's chosen field of study, either, and while he was not entirely ignorant of the subject, he couldn't for the life of him recall if there was a part of England that had once been known as Darn, with a kingdom in it ruled by a succession of monarchs named Frank. He knew that there had been a bunch of Richards, and a George or two, so it did not seem entirely unreasonable that a few Franks might have slipped in there somewhere.

He also knew that little was known about the very early history of England, when there were Celts and Picts and Druids and various other bogtrotters in the neighborhood. (Even Franks, for that matter, which probably only added to his confusion.) What little was known about this period had come down from the Romans, in the writings of people such as Julius Caesar, and unfortunately, Caesar had spent less time describing the various tribes and cultures he'd encountered than he did in describing how he butchered them. While this general lack of knowledge made for a good deal of leeway for writers of fantasy novels, it was not much help to Brewster. There were lots of legends, but unfortunately, little in the way of cold, hard facts.

Brewster believed that he had somehow traveled a lot further back in time than he'd intended, and that he was now stranded (temporarily, he hoped) in the early pagan days of England, when people had believed in such things as sorcerers and magic. As a result, Mick had erroneously assumed he was a sorcerer and Brewster had decided it would only complicate things unnecessarily if he attempted to disabuse him of that notion. (This was not, as it would turn out, a very wise decision, for it would lead to more complications than Brewster could imagine, but let's not get ahead of the story.)

As he sat there at the large, albeit very low, table in Mick's cottage, watching Mick wolfing down enough groceries to feed an average family of six for a week, Brewster did the best he could to give his host an explanation of his situation—or, at least, what he thought his situation was. (Now this was not an easy thing to do, so there's not much point in trying to reproduce the dialogue. To begin with, there was a lot of hemming and hawing and nervous throat clearing, as most scientists are not very good public speakers, and the conversation was interspersed with many interesting, if totally irrelevant, digressions, and explanations of the explanations, which in turn had to be explained, all of which was punctuated by the occasional rafter-rattling belch from Mick. Quite aside from all this, you saw what happened when we discussed time travel in Chapter One, and I'm sure you wouldn't want to go through *that* again.)

Suffice it to say that this discussion took a while, because time travel is difficult enough to explain to someone who's read science fiction novels and seen Steven Spielberg films, but Mick was a product of his world and of his time and, as such, did not possess those cultural advantages.

Well, you can probably guess what the result was. Aside from the fact that Mick became hopelessly confused, by the time Brewster was finished, the leprechaun believed more firmly than ever that Brewster was not only a master sorcerer, but quite possibly one of the greatest wizards of all time.

This is not an uncommon phenomenon. As most politicians, evangelists, and college professors know, if you really want to impress people with the magnitude of your intelligence and the scope of your abilities, the best thing you can do is to confuse them. If they can't make any sense of what you're saying, they're likely to assume it's way over their heads and that, consequently, you must be a genius, or at the very least an expert in your field.

Mick was no exception. He was pretty bright, and for a leprechaun, that's saying something, because while leprechauns don't have much in the way of formal education, they are the all-time champs at street smarts. Since Brewster, in trying to explain things to him, made no attempt to distinguish between sorcery and science, Mick came away from this discussion with a slightly distorted view of the actual facts. And the actual facts could be confusing enough all by themselves. (Remember when we covered Buckyballs back in Chapter One? You thought your narrator made that up, didn't you? Well, I didn't, but don't take my word for it. Ask Isaac Asimov about them, he knows everything. Anyway, imagine how it must have sounded to someone who had never even *heard* of science.)

To Mick, the whole thing clearly smacked of alchemy, which was his great passion, and even though he had trouble following Brewster's explanations, he was enormously impressed. Awed, in fact. For Brewster, as he now perceived him, was obviously not only a sorcerer of the first rank, but a master alchemist, as well. And if he was a master alchemist, that meant he had attained the goal that all alchemists devote their whole lives to pursuing—the secret of the Philosopher's Stone.

The secret of the Philosopher's Stone, you understand, was the alchemist's Holy Grail. (Actually, this is a rather faulty analogy, since the Holy Grail was the chalice used by Christ at the Last Supper and this is another universe entirely, so Mick wouldn't know the Holy Grail from a Dixie cup.) In the universe that Brewster came from, alchemists were wizards of a sort who played with rather primitive chemistry sets and sought the secret of changing base metals into gold. This was known as the secret of the Philosopher's Stone. (Don't ask why they referred to it this way, your narrator hasn't the faintest idea. Perhaps they thought that if they found just the right rock to toss into the athanor, this would turn the trick. Who knows?)

In any case, in this particular universe, gold was so common as to be relatively worthless. It could be found lying around all over the place, in almost every streambed and rock formation, and while it was rather pretty, it wasn't valuable at all. It was often used for plates and goblets and women sometimes used it for junk jewelry. (If Brewster had been less preoccupied, he might have noticed that his plate, his utensils, his teacup, and his saucer were all made of hammered gold, but then he hadn't noticed that the sun rose in the west and set in the east, either, which was definitely not the way things normally occurred.

The point being, in Mick's universe, the secret of the Philosopher's Stone did not refer to turning base metals into gold at all, because there was already plenty of the stuff around. The secret was jealously protected by the elite of the Sorcerers and Adepts Guild (commonly known as the

Guild or, simply, SAG). It involved a series of rather crude laboratory procedures and a whole slew of complicated incantations, the result of which was the creation of the most valuable metal in all the twenty-seven kingdoms—nickallirium.

Nickallirium was the rarest and most precious of all metals, since only sorcerers who were master alchemists could make it. Its chief virtues were that it was very light and strong, resistant to corrosion, and could easily be worked. It had a silvery color and was used chiefly as a medium of exchange. The coins made from nickallirium were very light, a serious consideration in an economy based entirely on cash and barter, and since only the elite of the Sorcerers and Adepts Guild had the secret of the Philosopher's Stone—that is, the secret of making nickallirium from base metals—they consequently had a lot of pull. (Monarchs had a tendency to be polite to wizards who could not only cast nasty spells at them, but who held the reins of the economy, as well. The combination was almost as dangerous as a congressman who also happens to be a lawyer.) As a result, the Guild was the single most powerful body in all the twenty-seven kingdoms, rather like the Teamsters.

The Guild was very protective of its power, and because of this, they had a certain way of doing things. Only dues-paying members of the Guild were entitled to represent themselves as sorcerers or adepts, and not just anyone could join. To begin with, a Guild member had to be human. (This was not actually written in the bylaws, as SAG did not wish to be accused of prejudice, but in practice, that was how it worked.) A prospective Guild member had to demonstrate a working knowledge of magic. (There was a test, complete with multiple choice and essay questions, at the end of which there was a lab quiz.) A prospective Guild member also had to have a sponsor who was already a dues-paying member of SAG, and he or she had to have served a period of apprenticeship with said sponsor, the duration of which was up to the sponsor's discretion. (In other words, you couldn't take the test until your sponsor decided you were ready.)

Ranking in the Guild was determined solely by the Guild Council, elected by master members of the Guild for life. (Rather like being a Supreme Court justice. Elections were held only when there was a vacancy, and a vacancy occurred only when there was a death. However, that happened fairly frequently, as the master members of the Guild were nothing if not competitive.) And the most jealously guarded secret of the Guild was the secret of the Philosopher's Stone.

The only way to learn the secret was to discover it for yourself and demonstrate it to the Council's satisfaction, which resulted in elevation to the rank of master alchemist and an appointment to the Ways and Means Committee. Only a mere handful of people knew the secret and Mick realized that if he was able to discover it, then according to their own bylaws, there was no way the Guild could deny him membership, even if he wasn't human. And more than anything, Mick longed to be a master alchemist.

The way Mick saw it, if he could convince Brewster to take him on as an apprentice, then he would have a sponsor, and that would get him over the first hurdle. Once Brewster accepted him as an apprentice, then perhaps he'd help him learn the secret of the Philosopher's Stone, which Mick was certain Brewster knew. And, in fact, he did. Brewster knew what nickallirium was, you see. He merely knew it by another name.

Aluminum.

Which explains why Mick was now staring at him with absolutely stunned, slack-jawed astonishment as Brewster removed a splinter he'd picked up in his palm from the rough surface of the wooden table. Mick was staring at his little tweezers, you see. Little tweezers made out of pure nickallirium, the rarest and most precious metal in the universe. (Mick's universe, that is. The mind boggles at what his reaction might have been if he could have seen a recycling compactor.) Moreover, these little tweezers had been produced out of a peculiar object the like of which Mick had never seen before in all his life. The peculiar object was Brewster's trusty little Swiss Army knife.

Now, to those of you who might be among the uninitiated few, those poor, deprived souls who have never had the pleasure of owning a genuine Swiss Army knife, it should be said that a Swiss Army knife is unquestionably one of the crowning achievements of human civilization. (They make neat little Christmas presents, too.) However, this is the sort of realization one comes to gradually.

A gift of a Swiss Army knife to someone who has never owned one before is quite likely to result in raised eyebrows and a somewhat awkward, "Oh. Gee . . . thanks. I've . . . uh . . . always wanted one of these." To which the correct response should be, "You're very welcome," and a knowing little smile. Because, you see, such an individual has not yet been enlightened. But enlightenment will come, don't worry. It may come soon, or it may take a little time, especially if the recipient of this bountiful gift thoughtlessly tucks it away inside a purse or a desk drawer and forgets about it for a while. However, it will come eventually, for sooner or later, that Swiss Army knife will be remembered and its skills brought into play.

Perhaps, as in Brewster's case at the moment, it will take a splinter that one needs tweezers to remove. Perhaps a cord on a package will need cutting, or a screw will require tightening when there is no toolbox handy, or a toothpick will be needed when there aren't any around, or there will arise a need for a handy pair of scissors and there will be no scissors to be found . . . but wait! Wasn't there a scissor blade on that Swiss Army knife? And then, once a person realizes just how useful this marvelous little piece of cutlery can be, they will never want to be without it.

They might even go out and buy a second one, with a different set of blades, because the one they've got doesn't have a saw or a magnifying glass, and there may arise a need to keep another in the toolbox or the kitchen drawer, one for the office, a tiny one to keep on a key chain, and so forth, until one is the proud owner of several of these wonderful contraptions and comes to a true appreciation of just how practical and useful they can be.

And then, when the ultimate stage of enlightenment is achieved, that individual starts handing out Swiss Army knives as gifts to friends and relatives, who will probably respond with raised eyebrows and an awkward, "Oh. Gee . . . thanks. I've . . . uh . . . always wanted one of these." But then, such is the nature of the benefits of advanced civilization. One doesn't always recognize them at first.

(You might think the preceding was a rather long and pointless expository lump, but rest assured, it wasn't. Actually, it was an intrusive narrative aside, but we'll leave such technical terms for graduate students and people who write literary criticism. The point is, it had a purpose. Quite aside from the fact that your narrator happens to be fond of knives, due to a rather troubled childhood, Swiss Army knives and the enlightening effect they have on people play an important part in Brewster's story. Remember, always trust your narrator.)

Now, where were we?

Oh, right. Brewster is sitting at a decimated smorgasbord and trying to remove a splinter from his palm with his trusty little pair of tweezers, while Mick is watching with amazement. Onward . . .

"There, that's got it," Brewster said, plucking out the splinter with his tweezers. He glanced up at Mick, saw the expression on his face, and frowned. "What is it?"

"Faith, and I was about to ask you that very thing," said Mick. "A wee pair of tongs, is it?"

"Oh, you mean these?" said Brewster. "They're called tweezers."

"Why?"

Brewster frowned again. "I'm not sure, exactly. Perhaps because women used them to pluck out their eyebrows."

Mick raised his. *"What?"*

"It was called tweezing, I think," said Brewster, uncertain because etymology was not his field of expertise, either. It occurred to him that for a scientist there was an awful lot of stuff he didn't know, but then, for a scientist, that sort of thought tends to be reassuring.

"Women actually *do* that in your Ing Land?" Mick said with amazement. "Whatever would a woman want to pluck her eyebrows out for?"

"Well, it used to be the fashion," Brewster replied. "But eyebrows are back in style again." He frowned. "Or at least they will be, in another few thousand years or so."

"Faith, and I've never heard the like of it!" said Mick. "But why is it that you have such a large sheath for such a wee little pair of tongs?"

"Hmmm?" said Brewster. "Oh, you mean this thing?" He smiled. "It's not a sheath. It's a Swiss Army knife."

He passed it across the table to Mick.

Now, this wasn't one of the cheaper models, but a deluxe one, with two regular knife blades, a screwdriver, a can opener, a bottle opener, a saw, a magnifying glass, a scissors, an awl, a corkscrew, a toothpick, and, of course, tweezers. In other words, the whole shebang. It had red plastic handles with the authentic Swiss cross emblem on one side that marked it as the genuine article. Mick, naturally, took it to be Brewster's crest.

He turned the knife over and over in his hands, and being both an armorer and a leprechaun, as well as an amateur alchemist (in other words, a fairly clever fellow), it didn't take him very long to figure out how it worked. He opened it and stared at each blade with speechless wonder.

One of the reasons for his speechlessness was the sheer ingenuity of the thing. As an armorer, he was immediately able to grasp its practicality. The other reason for his astonishment, aside from the tweezers made of nickallirium, was the material the blades were made of. Being an armorer, Mick knew a great deal about blades of all sorts. Most of his were made of iron, some were made of bronze, and a few—a very few—were made of steel. However, this was steel of a sort known in Brewster's universe as Damascus steel, highly prized for its strength and ability to hold an edge, and because it was so difficult to make. It took a master swordmaker, and a great deal of time, involving endless folding of the metal and lots of hammering and quenching and stuff like that (put it this way, it was complicated), and the result was a thing of beauty, a tempered blade that had colorful ripples running through it, due to the folding and layering process.

However, Brewster's knife was made of stainless steel, and consequently, there were no ripples in the surface of the blades. They were bright and smooth and sharp and shiny, which baffled Mick completely. No matter how closely he looked at the metal, he could not detect the slightest ripple or discoloration. He was thunderstruck.

"Truly, 'tis a thing of beauty!" he said with awe as he held the knife up to the light coming through the window.

"See how it gleams! I have never seen such craft in all my days! Who made this wondrous many-bladed knife for you?"

"Victorinox," said Brewster absently, taking a sip of tea.

"Then, truly, this Victorinox must be the greatest armorer in all the world!" said Mick as he stared at the knife with reverential respect. "Nay, no mere armorer, but a true artist! Oh, would that I could learn how to craft such a wondrous blade!"

"Oh, it shouldn't be really all that difficult," said Brewster casually.

Mick stared at him with disbelief. "Not difficult! Meanin' no offense, Doc, but I do not think you understand what it means to forge a blade. And a blade such as this . . ." Mick shook his head with humble admiration. "I know of no armorer anywhere in the twenty-seven kingdoms who could make such a blade!"

Brewster shrugged as he poured himself another cup of tea. "Well, I'm sure you're right, Mick, but it's just a matter of knowing how, you see. It really wouldn't be that complicated, actually." He pursed his lips, thoughtfully. "Of course, mass production would be rather difficult, but on a limited scale . . . why, yes, I don't see why it couldn't be done. The work would all have to be done by hand, of course, so it would be somewhat more time consuming, but not at all impossible."

Mick looked very dubious, but he also suddenly looked very interested. "You mean to tell me, Doc, that you would know how to make a many-bladed knife such as this?"

"Well, I'm not an armorer," Brewster admitted, "but then again, you are, and what I lack in specific knowledge of that craft, you could undoubtedly supply. Actually, it should prove rather interesting, as we would each bring certain skills to the project that the other could benefit from.

Hmmmm. As to making the steel itself, we probably couldn't match it exactly, because the manufacture of stainless steel would require a certain percentage of nickel, molybdenum, and chromium, which I rather doubt we could get our hands on, frankly, but although the technology of this era is primitive and crude, we do have the essentials.''

Brewster scratched his head absently as he considered the problem, while Mick watched and listened with growing interest.

"You already have pig iron," said Brewster, "I saw plenty of it in your smithy. And you have the basic knowledge, if you work with iron and bronze, and you have a forge . . . well, for our purposes, we'd need to make some modifications."

He scratched his head again and thought about it for a moment. "We would require, I think, a double action bellows, which we would need to power somehow . . . perhaps if there's a river or a stream nearby, we could harness water power. Of course, the bellows would have to be quite large, so we'd probably need more room than you've got in your smithy at the moment, but once we've got that, we could use the bellows to pump air by piston through a pipe up to the crucible. We'd have to construct some sort of ceramic pipe, I should imagine . . . And using coke for fuel, we should be able to melt the pig iron at fairly high temperatures, then add lime to remove the impurities, blow air over it to remove the carbon, pour it out into the proper molds . . . I imagine a wood mold would work reasonably well, not ideal, perhaps, but it should do . . . and then it would be merely a matter of finishing the blade, which means we'd have to polish and sharpen it before it's tempered, that way you wouldn't break the crystals when you sharpened it, you see, and it would hold an edge better. Then we heat it up again and drop it in oil, followed by a final polish to remove the oil from the top layer . . . which means we'd probably need a wheel, I suppose . . . and what we'd get should be a pretty good grade of steel. Of course, it would rust unless it were properly taken care of, but otherwise, it would be just about the same. We'd simply use different molds for the desired blade shapes and flat springs, then rivet the pieces together, come up with some kind of suitable material for the handles . . . and there you'd have it.''

Mick stared at him with new respect as Brewster, the problem theoretically solved, removed his pipe from his jacket pocket and started filling it with tobacco.

"You never said you were a smith, as well!'' said Mick with amazement.

"Well, I'm not,'' said Brewster, "but we're really only dealing with some basic principles here. You'd know about the smithing part, and the rest of it would simply be a matter of some elementary engineering.''

"And you could show me how to perform this . . . engineerin'?'' Mick said, thinking it must be some sort of spell.

"No problem,'' Brewster said. He patted his pockets for his lighter, but apparently, he had either forgotten it or lost it in the crash.

"Allow me,'' said Mick, who was picking his teeth with a sharpened twig. While Brewster continued searching his pockets for the lighter, Mick held the twig out, mumbled a fire spell, and the twig burst into flame.

"Oh, thanks,'' said Brewster absently, drawing on the pipe as Mick held the burning twig to the tobacco.

CHAPTER
FOUR

By now, you're probably thinking, Now wait a minute . . . Doesn't Brewster realize that by introducing technology into the past, much less into an entirely different universe, he's interfering with history and incurring all the risks that implies?

Well, in a word, no.

For one thing, Brewster still hasn't figured out that he's in another universe. (Give him time. He's actually doing pretty well, all things considered.) For another, scientists often tend to be rather literal-minded, and when presented with a problem, they simply consider that problem in terms of a solution. (Remember the Manhattan Project?)

Scientists love problems, and Brewster was certainly no exception. He became caught up in Mick's enthusiasm and did not really pause to consider all the ramifications of what he was about to do. This is not at all unusual. It is extremely doubtful that Dr. Victor Frankenstein, for instance, paused to consider all the ramifications of creating life before he embarked upon his famous project. (For that matter, some people argue that the Creator did not really pause to consider all the ramifications of creating life. Such people are called philosophers.) In any case, it never even occurred to Brewster that he might be meddling with history, or playing around with things "man was not meant to know," or any of that negative existential stuff. Like countless scientists and tinkerers before him, who might have thought twice had they paused to consider what innovations such as television, nuclear energy, or microchips might lead to, he simply considered the problem in terms of a solution, scratched his head, and solved it.

In theory, that is.

In practice, of course, it was somewhat more complicated, and the moment Brewster realized that Mick was seriously interested in actually *doing* it, why then, it became another interesting problem—the problem of putting theory into practice, which is something else scientists dearly love to do. They will blissfully go through life solving problem after problem, something they have in common with engineers, and as long as they're kept busy, they'll be happy. (Trust me, you really don't want to have scientists with nothing but time on their hands. When that happens, they start writing novels.)

The immediate problem, of course, was finding a suitable location for the project, as Mick's smithy—despite being built to accommodate his normal-sized customers—was much too small. Mick, however, had a perfect solution to the problem.

"I know just the place," he said as they walked the trail leading out from behind his little cottage to the foothills. "As it happens, I'd already considered offerin' its use to you."

He paused to yank on the rope he held in his hand. Tethered at the other end of the rope was the little peregrine bush. Brewster had never seen anyone walk a bush on a leash before, but Mick explained that he did it every day. Most of the time, he kept the bush inside the smithy, where he was afraid it did not get enough light. Taking it for walks helped, but Mick had to use the leash, not so much because he was afraid the bush would wander off, for it didn't move too quickly, but because it had a tendency to burrow its roots into the ground if left alone and then it was a pain to dig it up again.

"You never know," said Mick, once he got the bush moving again, "it might take a while to find this other missin' magic chariot of yours, and while I would be honored to have you for a house guest, my humble cottage is really much too small for your proper comfort and the smithy wouldn't do at all, y'see. Nay, I have just the place in mind. My laboratory would suit our purpose admirably, I think."

Brewster's ears perked up and he stopped on the trail. "Excuse me, but did you say . . . laboratory?"

"Aye," Mick replied, stopping as well. "I'm a student of the art of alchemy, y'know. I thought I'd mentioned that."

"Oh. Well, you probably did," said Brewster. "You'll have to excuse me, I tend to be a bit distracted sometimes."

"Sure, and I understand," said Mick. "A man like yourself has a great many important things to think about."

There was a scratching sort of sound and Mick gave the rope another violent tug. "Don't you start!" he snapped as the bush started burrowing its roots into the ground. "Stop that, you miserable shrub!"

The bush stopped its burrowing and its leaves seemed to droop.

"I've never seen anything like that," Brewster said, watching the peregrine bush with fascination.

"Bloody stupid sprout," Mick mumbled irritably, giving the rope another tug.

Unaccountably, Brewster found himself feeling sorry for the bush. "There, that's all right," he said in a soothing tone as he leaned over the bush. "He didn't really mean it."

"Sure, and you don't think it understands you?" Mick said, looking at Brewster with a puzzled expression. "It's just a bloody bush, y'know."

"Well, maybe not," said Brewster, "but Pamela always speaks kindly to her plants and they seem to grow very nicely for her."

"I never heard of such a thing," said Mick. "Pamela. Is she your wench?"

"Aye," said Brewster. "Uh, that is, I mean, yes, she's my fiancée."

"Well, fancy or not, I've never met a wench yet who spoke to plants and trees and such, unless she was a dryad. Is she a dryad, then?"

"No, she's Protestant."

"Faith, and I don't envy you, if she goes around protestin' and wearin' masks and speakin' to shrubbery. Still," he added hastily, not wishing to give offense, "I'm sure she has other fine and admirable qualities."

"Uh . . . yes," said Brewster, deciding to change the subject. "Look, when you say 'laboratory,' what exactly do you mean? What sort of laboratory?"

"Oh, y'know, the place where I keep all my alchemical apparatus," Mick replied. "My athanor, my potions, my tinctures and instruments and furnace, all that sort of thing."

"Ah, I see," said Brewster, not really seeing at all. "But you *do* have a furnace?" That part, at least, he understood.

"Oh, aye," said Mick. "And there's a stream runnin' past it, out back, which you said you required."

"Hmmm," said Brewster, mulling this information over as they walked the path through the tiny woods. The bush rustled along behind them, and perhaps Brewster only imagined it, but it seemed to him that its leaves had perked up a bit after he'd spoken nicely to it. "Exactly how far away from your laboratory is this stream?"

"Oh, it's right there, as soon as you poke your head out the back door," said Mick. "At one time, a wizard must have made his home there, for when I found it, the alchemical apparatus was still there, only all put away inside a storage chamber where it was gatherin' dust. At some time after the wizard left, y'see, somebody came along and decided the place would make a fine location for a mill, so they took all the alchemical apparatus and put it away. Probably afraid to muck about with it too much. Then they went and built themselves a water wheel and set up the grindin' stone and—"

"What's that? You say there's a water wheel?" Brewster interrupted with sudden interest. He'd been getting a bit lost with all this talk of alchemy and wizards.

"Oh, aye," said Mick. "Great, big, bloody thing. Had to be big to turn the millstone, y'see."

"Hmmm. What kind of condition is it in?" asked Brewster. "I mean, is it still in a decent state of repair?"

"Oh, aye, that it is," said Mick with an emphatic nod. "I open up the sluice gate and give it a go when it comes harvest time. McMurphy and the other farmers hereabouts bring me their grain to mill in exchange for some of their produce. Whoever built it did a right proper job, they did. Redwood construction, through and through. Good craftsmanship, and that redwood lasts forever, y'know."

"Hmmm," said Brewster. "How much farther is it?"

"Oh, it's right up ahead," said Mick, "just around the next bend."

They turned a bend in the trail and came to a large clearing. Brewster stopped short and simply stared. "Good Lord," he said. "Will you look at that?"

"Aye, but I've already seen it, y'know," Mick replied, somewhat puzzled.

Standing at the far end of the clearing, not quite fifty yards away, was an old stone keep built somewhat in the Norman style. There were remnants of a wall running around it, but most of the wall had long since crumbled, or perhaps been battered down at some point in the past. The ruins of it were not much more than waist high except in one or two places. Beyond the wall was the keep itself, dominated by a square stone tower that stood four stories high, with crenellations at the top.

Attached to the tower was a lower structure only one story high, also constructed of stone, with a flat roof. The shape of the entire keep was that of an "L" lying on its side. Built onto the side of the lower structure, where the stream had been channeled to run past it, was a gigantic wooden water wheel. At one time, there must have been a moat around the walls, drawing its water from the stream, but it had been filled in at some point, perhaps when the keep had been converted to a mill and there was no more use for it.

"Why, it's wonderful!" said Brewster, thinking that it looked rather like a small-scale version of Frankenstein's castle.

Mick beamed. "I'm pleased you like it," he replied. "Of course, 'tis a wee bit tumble-down in spots, but some fixin' up and it should be as good as new. I haven't put much work in it, y'see. Still, the tower would make a right fine residence, it would. Runnin' water, nice property, and a pretty good view, to boot. Care to have a look inside?"

"Oh, absolutely," Brewster said, his enthusiasm mounting.

They crossed the clearing and went through the space in the ruins of the wall where the gates must have once been. Brewster could see from the unevenness of the ground where the moat had been filled in. Much of the grounds of the keep were overgrown, with tall grass and bushes and a few young saplings here and there. As they approached, Brewster could see that the structure, while obviously neglected for some years, nevertheless appeared to be quite sound.

The stream running past the keep and around behind it was actually a good-sized creek running down from the mountains, and the water babbled swiftly along the rocky streambed. The huge wooden water wheel stood still and Brewster could see that the sluice gate controlling the flow to it was closed. But what struck him most was the color of the wheel itself.

"Why is it red?" he asked, puzzled.

Mick raised his eyebrows. "Why, because 'tis redwood," he replied. "I thought I'd mentioned that."

Brewster frowned. "So you did," he admitted.

He moved up for a closer look and saw that the wheel was neither stained nor painted, for neither would have held up over time, but that the wood itself seemed to be naturally red. A sort of bright crimson color, and rather attractive, too.

"Redwood," he mumbled to himself.

"Aye, sure," said Mick, noticing the way Brewster was staring at the wheel. "We're in the middle of a whole forest of it. Y'mean to tell me that you've never seen redwood before? Doesn't redwood grow in Ing Land?"

Brewster frowned. "No, come to think of it, it doesn't."

He scratched his head. It seemed to him that the only redwood forest he had ever heard of was in California. He had been to California only twice, the first time to visit Los Angeles for a conference at UCLA, and the second to visit the Jet Propulsion Laboratories. He had never actually seen a redwood tree, except in photographs. He recalled the trees being seriously huge, and while the trees around them were, indeed, extremely large and very tall, they looked more like English oaks than redwoods.

He could not recall the wood underneath the bark of redwood trees actually being red in color. Certainly, not *that* shade of red. He was reasonably sure that it was only vaguely reddish. This was quite a different hue, much brighter, almost as red as blood.

"Hmmm," said Brewster, scratching his head some more. "Strange."

"What?" Mick asked.

"Oh, nothing, I was merely thinking out loud," Brewster said, deciding to mull things over for a while. He had learned long ago that this was a good way to keep from looking foolish.

Clearly, there were some puzzling aspects to this predicament, but there was a lot he didn't really know yet. Such as where he was, exactly, and what year it was, little things like that. Make no conclusions until all the facts are in, he reminded himself, recalling the words of his high school physics teacher. Still, migratory bushes and redwood trees in England? It certainly was puzzling. It made no sense whatsoever. Perhaps he was in Ireland.

They went inside the keep for a look around and Brewster felt as if he'd stepped onto a movie set. The first floor of the tower was taken up by a large, open chamber that was a sort of great hall, only it wasn't very great. It was rather smallish. It had a beamed ceiling and a stone floor, and the walls were also made of stone, of course. It had a huge fireplace and a thirty-foot ceiling, taking up the first two stories of the tower.

There was a second inner wall constructed about twelve feet in from the outer wall, forming a corridor running all the way around the main chamber. A large archway led to the lower structure attached to the tower. The inner corridor gave access to two flights of stone steps, one near the front and one at the back, which led up to a gallery that ran all the way around the main chamber, where the second floor would have been. There were several small archways leading from the corridor on the first floor to the main chamber. The archways on the gallery were roughly in line with the small, high windows in the outer wall, allowing some light to reach the main chamber. Still, it was rather dark and gloomy. There were sconces in the wall for torches, with the walls above and behind them blackened by flames.

The furnishings were rather Spartan, merely a couple of long, heavy wooden tables and benches made from planks, with a third, smaller table and bench on a slightly raised stone dais near the far wall. Brewster ran his finger through the thick layer of dust on one of the tables.

"As I said, I haven't really done much to the place," said Mick. "Hardly ever come in here. Spend most of my time in the laboratory, y'know."

"Can we see that next?" asked Brewster.

"Sure, and I'd be proud to show it to you," Mick said.

They went through the large archway into the lower structure, which was divided into three smaller chambers. The first and largest held the millstone, which was driven by a primitive pair of large wooden gear wheels. One wooden gear wheel was mounted vertically, on a large wooden shaft that was turned directly by the water wheel. Its heavy wooden pegs meshed with the second gear wheel, which was mounted horizontally on the shaft that turned the millstone. It was engineering at its most basic, Brewster noted, but it worked.

The second chamber held Mick's laboratory, which bore no resemblance whatsoever to any laboratory Brewster had ever seen. There were several long wooden tables made of planks, with benches and small stools behind them, and the walls were lined with crudely constructed wooden shelves that held small ceramic pots, cloudy glass jars of various shapes and sizes, and a wide assortment of metallic vessels. There were glass pipettes and blocks, a stock of bronze and pig iron, some gold and silver ingots, and a wide variety of mineral samples of all sorts. One entire section of shelving appeared to be full of nothing but rocks and crystals.

The tops of the tables were cluttered with more of these mineral samples, more glass and ceramic jars, blackened iron pots and kettles and various utensils, and iron dishes in which the residue of partially burned substances resided like solidified sludge. There were several small hand bellows for puffing air onto the flames of whatever noxious mixtures Mick burned in those pots and kettles and there were mortars and pestles for grinding things up into a powder.

The floor of the ''laboratory,'' aside from being littered with the debris of Mick's experiments, was almost completely covered with wooden buckets and wicker baskets full of dirt-encrusted rocks of all kinds, scummy water and broken glass and pot shards. There was a crude, heavy furnace in one corner and a small writing table with a slanted top and little cubbyholes containing rolled up vellum scrolls. There was also a large, iron-banded wooden chest with a crude-looking lock on it placed against the back wall. It looked just like the chests pirates often used for buried treasure.

''Well, what do you think?'' asked Mick, picking his way through the clutter to the center of the room, where he stood proudly and possessively, with his hands on his hips.

Brewster wasn't quite sure what to say. ''It's, uh . . . certainly impressive.''

Mick beamed.

''It looks like you've been busy,'' Brewster added.

''Haven't had all that much success, really,'' Mick said. ''Still, I come here every chance I have and putter about.''

"What have you got locked up in the chest?" asked Brewster.

"Don't really know," Mick replied with a shrug. "I've never had it open. Don't have the key, y'know, and 'tis a shame to break open a perfectly good lock. Aside from that, you never know what might be in there. If a wizard goes and locks something up, perhaps it should remain that way."

"Mmmm," said Brewster, thinking that the primitive lock really wouldn't be very difficult to pick.

"You'll most likely find all you need here," Mick said proudly.

Brewster glanced about dubiously. "No doubt," he said, not wishing to hurt Mick's feelings. "Should we see the rest of the place?"

The third and final chamber was largely empty except for a number of large wooden casks stacked up against the wall and a huge, flame-blackened iron kettle.

"This is where I store the wine," Mick explained. "Not much left now. These casks are mostly empty. Brigands took almost the entire last batch I brewed. Seems I can never make enough."

"How do you make it?" Brewster asked.

"Ah, well, I cook up the roots in that big kettle there until I have a good mash," Mick explained. "Then I let it cool and add a bit o' the last batch to get things started. I put it in the casks and store it in a root cellar I have out back, by the stream, where it keeps nice and cool. In the winter, I take it out and open up the casks, so I can skim the ice off the top each mornin' till it doesn't freeze, and then 'tis done."

"Hmmm, your basic cold brewing," Brewster said. "It must be very time consuming."

"Aye, but 'tis the only way," said Mick.

"Well, actually, there's a much easier way," Brewster replied. "You could make a still."

"A still what?" asked Mick.

"No, still is what it's called," Brewster explained. He saw Mick's frown and added, "It's short for distillery . . . an apparatus for brewing. It would greatly speed up the process and allow you to have a greater yield."

"Would it now?" said Mick with interest. "And how does one construct such an apparatus?"

"Well . . ." Brewster scratched his head and thought a moment. "I suppose we could make a fairly primitive, albeit functional, still without too much difficulty. We'd need a big metal pot . . . like that big kettle there . . . and then we'd need a smaller pot that could fit inside it, with pegs to keep it off the bottom, and a heavy lid, so we could put water in the big pot around it. Now in this lid, we'd have to have a piece of copper tubing . . . well, that could pose a problem, but I suppose we could fashion some, if we had the copper . . ."

"Aye, I have plenty of copper," Mick said excitedly. "Go on. What then?"

"Well, we'd make a tube rising up from the lid for, oh, about a foot or so, maybe a little more"—Brewster indicated the approximate measurement by holding his hands apart—"and at the top we would attach a second piece of tubing that's been wound in a coil. We would have water pouring over this coiled tubing . . . I suppose something as simple as a couple of leaky buckets would do the trick . . . and at the bottom of the coil, we'd stretch it out and run it into a container. You'd heat the water in the big pot, only you wouldn't want it to boil, you understand, just keep it warm and steaming, so it condenses out. That way, you could make your brew anytime you wanted, and you could make a lot more of it, and in a lot less time."

"S'trewth!" said Mick. "And you could show me how to make such a still apparatus?"

Brewster shrugged. "I don't see why not. It really isn't very complicated."

"Sure, and 'twould be a great boon to me if you could teach me this thing," Mick said with wonder. "And we'd split the profits, of course."

"Well, I'm not really interested in that," Brewster said. "It's the least I could do to repay you for your hospitality. And if you can help me find my other, uh, magic chariot...."

"I'll see to it the word is spread," Mick assured him emphatically. "In the meantime, you'll need a proper place to stay. Come on, then, I'll show you the rest o' the place."

They went back into the main chamber, where Mick tied the bush to one of the bench legs. Brewster followed him up the flight of steps to the gallery, then on to the third floor. There wasn't very much to see. A large room with a wood plank floor laid over the beams, another fireplace, another crudely made wooden table and two benches, and some ancient, torn, and moth-eaten tapestries hanging on the walls. There were mouse droppings on the floor and lots of cobwebs.

"Very nice," said Brewster with a wan grimace.

"Oh, perhaps 'tisn't much now," said Mick placatingly, "but a bit of cleanin' up and some new wall hangin's and you'd be surprised at what a difference 'twould make."

"I'm sure," said Brewster dubiously.

"And now, the top floor," Mick said, heading for the stairs.

"Penthouse suite," Brewster mumbled as he followed Mick.

The fourth floor of the tower was also a large, open room, similar to the one below, only with one difference. It had a bed. Or rather, what was left of one, which was little more than a crude, dilapidated wooden frame.

"All the comforts of home," Brewster mumbled.

"I can fix up that bed as good as new, never fear," Mick assured him. "But look at the view, eh?"

Brewster looked out the window. "Very nice."

" 'Tis even better up top," said Mick.

"Up top?"

"Aye, come on," said Mick, going up a narrow flight of stone steps at the back of the room.

Brewster followed him up to the top of the tower and out onto the battlement.

"Well, it *is* a rather nice view," Brewster admitted, looking out over the wall. "And I can see company coming."

"Aye, you can easily see anyone approachin' from up here," said Mick.

"No, I mean I can see company coming, right now," Brewster said, pointing.

Mick looked in the direction he was indicating, where two figures had just come out of the woods and were crossing the clearing.

"Sure, and 'tis Robie McMurphy, as I live and breathe," he said with a frown. "And that great, big, lumberin' oaf with him can be none other than Bloody Bob. Ach! He'll be needin' a new sword again, I'll wager. This'll be the fourth time since last winter."

The two figures stopped just inside the ruins of the wall and the man Mick identified as Bloody Bob put his cupped hands up to his mouth and called out in a deep basso voice that was loud enough to raise the dead, *"Ey, Mick! Mick O'Fallon!"*

"Come on, then," Mick said with a sigh. "We'd best get down there before that great oaf's yellin' makes the mortar crack."

They hurried downstairs.

"Best let me do most o' the talkin'," Mick said as they descended the stairs. "Bobby's got himself a nasty temper, he has. 'Tis on account of his infirmity, y'see. Best make no mention of it."

"What sort of infirmity?" asked Brewster.

"He's blind as a bat, he is," Mick replied. "Bob was a fearsome warrior in his time, y'see, but now he's with the brigands. Still strong as a bull, but he's gettin' on and he doesn't see so well now, though he flat refuses to admit it. Goes around squintin' all the time and knockin' into trees, then challengin' them to fight him. Can't see much past his big red nose."

"So then he's nearsighted?" Brewster said.

"Aye, I suppose 'tis one way you can put it," Mick agreed, having never heard the term before. "Sees only what's near him, and that none too well. But makin' mention of it only goads him to a bloody fury, and that's right dangerous. But he'll suffer more from me than others, on account of I make wine for the brigands and they need my services as an armorer, y'see. Especially old Bob. He's one of my best customers, though 'tis a cryin' shame the way he keeps losin' the perfectly good swords I make for him."

By this time, they'd reached the ground floor and come out through the front door. Standing a short distance in front of them were Robie McMurphy and the biggest, most fearsome-looking man Brewster had ever seen.

Bloody Bob stood close to seven feet tall and weighed three hundred pounds or more. His chest was massive, his arms were huge, and his girth was considerable, as well. His physical dimensions were formidable enough, but his appearance made him look even more frightening. Most of his face was covered by a huge gray beard and his graying hair was worn down to his shoulders. He had a weathered, ruddy complexion and a large scar on the side of his face, partly hidden by the beard. His hands were huge, easily twice the size of Brewster's, and looked perfectly capable of crushing skulls. He wore chain mail over a leather jerkin, a metal helmet with a spike on top, old buckskin trousers, and knee-high, laced leather moccasins. Brewster thought he looked like a cross between a Viking and a Hell's Angel.

"McMurphy said you might be here, Mick," rumbled Bloody Bob.

"Aye, I'm here," said Mick. "What is it you'll be needin' from me?"

The huge man looked a bit embarrassed as he towered over little Mick. He shuffled a foot and cleared his throat, a sound similar to that made by a bear with a lousy disposition.

"I'll be needin' a new sword, Mick."

"And what happened to the last one that I made for you?" Mick asked, a touch belligerently.

"Uh . . . somebody must have stolen it."

"Stolen it, you say? And who, might I ask, would have the temerity to steal from a great, big, overblown bear such as yourself, eh?"

"I dunno, Mick. If I'd have caught the blackguard, I'd have torn him limb from limb, I would have, but 'twas some dastardly footpad made off with it."

"A footpad, was it? The last time 'twas a burglar, was it not?"

"Aye, a burgler," the big man said, nodding emphatically.

"And what might be the difference 'twixt a footpad and a burglar?"

Bloody Bob frowned. "Well, uh . . . one's a footpad . . . and one's a burglar."

"Aye, and the last time before that 'twas a thief."

"Uh . . . I believe 'twas, aye."

"A thief, and then a burglar, and then a footpad," Mick said sarcastically. "You seem to be plagued by criminals these days. Faith, and I don't know what the world is comin' to when you can't even trust your fellow brigands."

"Aye, 'tis a terrible thing," said Bob, nodding.

"Oh, come on now, Bobby, tell the truth," said Mick. "You lost it again, didn't you?"

"Uh, no, Mick, 'twas a thief . . ."

"You mean a footpad."

"Aye, a footpad."

It seemed strangely incongruous and almost comical to Brewster that such an imposing and fearsome-looking giant should be so deferential to a man who barely stood higher than his kneecaps, and yet Bloody Bob stood there, squinting down and shuffling his foot in the dirt and looking very much abashed.

"A footpad, my buttocks," Mick repeated wryly. He sighed. "I don't know what I'm goin' to do with you, Bobby. I keep makin' great big blades for you and you keep losin' them. You know how much work goes into making a sword for a great big oaf the likes of you?"

"I know, Mick, I know," Bloody Bob said apologetically. "I'm right sorry about this, I am. But I'm needin' another sword, Mick. Please?"

"Please, he says." Mick glanced over at Brewster with a long-suffering expression. "What's a body to do, Doc, eh?"

Bloody Bob peered around, squinting hard. "There somebody with you, Mick? Where's he hidin'? Tell him to come out, I won't be hurtin' him if he's a friend of yours."

"Why, he's standin' right in front of you, you great ox!" said Mick with exasperation.

"Oh, so he is," said Bloody Bob, squinting even harder and obviously not seeing a thing.

Mick rolled his eyes. "Say hallo to my friend, Brewster Doc, Bob. And be civil about it, mind you."

"Pleased to meet you," Bloody Bob said, sticking out his hand. The effect was somewhat spoiled by the fact that he held his hand out in a direction about two feet to one side of where Brewster was standing.

Brewster obligingly moved to where he could shake the big man's hand. Once again, he was clasped around the forearm instead of by the hand, and he returned the grip.

"He's a sorcerer," McMurphy whispered.

Immediately, Bloody Bob stiffened, and probably by reflex, his grip on Brewster's arm briefly tightened to the point of pain before he let go abruptly.

"A sorcerer!"

"Aye," said Mick, "so you be on your best behavior, hear?"

"Call me Doc," said Brewster. "Could I ask you to bend over a bit?"

Bloody Bob looked puzzled. "Bend over?"

"Yes, just bend down toward me a little."

"You won't be puttin' a spell on me, will you?"

"No, no, I just want to see something."

"Do as the man says, Bobby," Mick said, clearly wondering what Brewster had in mind.

Hesitantly, the big man bent down toward Brewster, who reached into the inside pocket of his jacket and took out his horn-rimmed glasses. He was nearsighted, as well, but though he often wore contacts because Pamela liked him better without his horn-rimmed frames, he never went anywhere without his glasses. He'd lost his contacts on more than one occasion.

He slipped the glasses onto Bloody Bob's face. "Try that," he said.

The big man's eyes suddenly grew very wide and Brewster

could see that they were a startling bright blue. Bloody Bob's jaw dropped in amazement.

"*S'trewth!*" he exclaimed.

"Is that any better?" Brewster asked him.

"I can *see!*" said Bloody Bob, glancing all around him.

"How well?" asked Brewster. "I mean, is your vision sharp now or are things a little vague and blurry?"

The big man gazed at him with awe. "I can see you well enough, Sorcerer," he replied, "but in the distance, things still look as if I'd had too much to drink. Yet, truly, I never thought to see this well again! 'Tis a wonder to behold!"

He took off the glasses and held them gently, staring at them reverently, then put them back on again and held his breath with astonishment.

"'Tis a *magic visor!*" he said. "I would give anything for such a wonder!"

"Well..." said Brewster, "that, uh, 'magic visor' is mine, but I think we might be able to make you one of your own. I saw some glass blocks in Mick's laboratory back there, and if we could make the right sort of wheel, I could try grinding up some lenses for you. It would have to be a process of trial and error, you understand. We'll probably have to make several pairs before we get it right, because I'm not an optometrist and there's no way I can establish a prescription. Still, with your help and a bit of luck, I'm sure we could improve your vision beyond what it is now."

"And what would you be askin' of me for such a wondrous boon?" asked Bloody Bob. "Name your price, Sorcerer, and I shall pay it if it takes a lifetime!"

"Well..." said Brewster, "I'm a stranger here and, uh, I could use some help..."

The giant dropped down to one knee and bowed his head. "I will serve you faithfully, Great Wizard, if you would help me to regain my sight."

"Sure, and I think you've made a friend for life, Doc," Mick said.

There was a clattering, banging sound and they turned to see the peregrine bush come rustling out through the front door, still tied to the wooden bench and dragging it along. It came up to Brewster, stopped, and raised its branches toward him.

"Two friends," said Mick wryly. "An ox and a shrub."

"Three," said Brewster, putting his hand on Mick's shoulder.

"Nay, four!" said McMurphy.

Brewster grinned and clasped forearms with the farmer. "Well, now we're getting somewhere," he said. "Come on, then. We've got a lot of work to do!"

CHAPTER
<u>FIVE</u>

Arthur C. Clarke once said that any sufficiently advanced technology would seem like sorcery to those who didn't understand it. (That was only a paraphrase, of course. Clarke said it a lot more elegantly, which is why he gets the big bucks.) And it's quite true. It is an inescapable fact of human nature that we often tend to fear that which we do not understand, or at the very least, we respond to it with a disquieting uneasiness. And it was with a disquieting uneasiness that Brewster's newfound friends regarded him, for while he seemed to be a nice enough fella, he was also one heck of an adept, as far as they were concerned. They knew enough about adepts to treat them with respect. Even to fear them. Some of them were downright terrifying.

Brewster didn't know it yet, but he was not the only sorcerer around, even if he was the only one in the general vicinity. (He had yet to learn about the Guild, but we're getting ahead of the story again.) Mick, as we have seen, has some slight skill with magic, but not because he is a sorcerer (which requires years of disciplined study and staying up nights cramming for exams). It's because he's fey. This is a characteristic shared by all leprechauns and nymphs and fairies (and to some extent, by elves), and it does not, as is often supposed, refer to campy mannerisms, but to being touched by enchantment. (If you don't believe me, look it up. I'll wait.)

When a human is said to be fey, it means that person has a sensitivity to things that are magical—which, perhaps, is why some people see such things as ghosts and others don't. Otherwise, the term means that enchantment is inherent in the creature itself. Mick, being a leprechaun, possessed some inborn magical abilities, but his abilities were little more than parlor tricks compared to what a *real* sorcerer could do. (Natural talent is all well and good, but it's no substitute for hard work, training, and experience. So stay in school, kids, do your homework, and don't goof off in study hall. The preceding has been a public service message from your narrator.)

Since he was unable to distinguish between sorcery and science, Mick was convinced that Brewster's knowledge of the thaumaturgic arts was quite extensive. Robie McMurphy was equally impressed, but no one was more overwhelmed than Bloody Bob, for in loaning him his glasses—or, as Bloody Bob put it, his "magic visor"—Brewster had temporarily restored to him his sight. As it happened, while Brewster's prescription lenses were not exactly right for Bloody Bob, they did improve his vision significantly. Of course, in Bloody Bob's case, just about anything short of a blindfold would have been a significant improvement.

Now, while Bloody Bob was not the brightest brigand in the forest, by any stretch of the imagination, he was undoubtedly the biggest and the strongest. In his younger days, he had been a very famous warrior, feared and respected throughout all the twenty-seven kingdoms. However, that was a long time ago and people have short

memories. (Just ask Mark Spitz.) The days when Bloody
Bob was eagerly sought after by every kingdom and duke-
dom and offered substantial salaries, profit sharing, great
benefits, and Beltane bonuses were long gone and now only
the old-timers remembered who he was. And most of them
thought that he was dead. He wasn't dead, but he had
foolishly neglected to put anything aside for his retirement.
This meant he had to work. Unfortunately, there wasn't
much work available for a man his age (which was probably
around sixty or so, he wasn't sure himself), nor for a man
who couldn't see the broad side of a barn, much less hit it.

This dearth of employment opportunities had left him
with few options. He had tried working as a bouncer in a
series of seedy little taverns, but due to his failing eyesight,
he kept bouncing the wrong people and was, in turn,
bounced himself (which resulted in a number of taverns
being forced to close down temporarily for renovation). Bob
had slowed down some in his old age, and he couldn't see
well, but he was still as strong as an elephant and he
angered quickly and easily. Pretty soon, word got around
and no one wanted to hire this nearsighted, albeit highly
dangerous, old man. So, having run out of options, Bloody
Bob turned to a life of crime.

He fell in with the Forest Brigands (back when they still
made their headquarters in the forest) and finally found a
situation where his abilities were properly appreciated. It
wasn't a *great* job, but it was okay. There wasn't very much
money to be made in the brigand trade, at least, not until
Black Shannon took over and brought her managerial skills
to the operation, but Bob was able to get by and he enjoyed
the camaraderie.

Brigands have always been, by nature, a rather rough-
and-tumble lot, and many of them were ex-warriors like
Bob, who were getting on in years, so they were able to

trade lots of old war stories. (In some cases, they'd fought for opposing sides, but it was only business, so no one had any hard feelings.) The younger brigands were generally warrior wannabe types who'd failed to make the grade for one reason or another, but they knew enough to show proper respect to the old troopers. (And if they didn't, they generally learned fairly quickly.) So, all things considered, Bloody Bob was pretty happy with his lot in life. He could have done much worse. However, his failing eyesight had been a source of considerable anguish to him. (Imagine how you'd feel if you could once bend a longbow and hit the bull's-eye every time from a hundred yards, only now you couldn't even see the target unless you were close enough to touch it.)

Worst of all for Bloody Bob was the embarrassment, the sheer mortification, of losing his swords. To a true warrior, nothing was more important than his sword. He ate with it, he slept with it, but he never, *ever* misplaced it. It was the worst possible sin. And Bob had done it more than once. He couldn't help it. He'd put his sword down somewhere and then be unable to find it again because he couldn't see well enough. The other brigands had learned to be considerate and if they happened upon his missing blade, they'd surreptitiously place it within his reach and then arrange for him to notice it.

("Ooops! Sorry, Bob. Didn't mean to trip over your sword. Didn't see it lying on the floor there, right next to your chair. Nay, on the other side of your chair, Bob.")

However, when it happened in the woods, or on the trail, or while he was taking a bath in a stream, there was no hope for it. He'd crawl about on his hands and knees, desperately feeling around for it, racking his brain to remember where he'd put it down, but almost invariably, he'd never find it, even if it was only a few feet away. The humiliation was unendurable. He could take growing old. He could take getting fat. He could even take irregularity and the painful itch of hemorrhoids, but he could not take having his eyesight fail him. Then, suddenly, out of nowhere, Brewster had come and shown him a miracle.

If Brewster had saved his life, if he had fixed him up with the most gorgeous woman who had ever lived, or if he'd given him the winning ticket to the Irish Sweepstakes, he could not have inspired greater devotion. From the moment Brewster placed his horn-rimmed glasses on Bloody Bob's red nose, he became the center of the old warrior's universe.

The keep soon became the hub of frenetic activity. First, of course, it was necessary to clean up the place and make it a suitable residence for a sorcerer of Brewster's stature. Mick busied himself with the construction of new furniture while Bloody Bob and Robie McMurphy pitched in to help sweep out the cobwebs and the mouse droppings.

McMurphy was eager to get in on the ground floor, so to speak, because Mick had shown him the Swiss Army knife and told him about their plans. McMurphy knew a good money-making opportunity when he saw one. They had a working mill, and a soon-to-be-expanded brewery, a smithy and an armory business, the proposed many-bladed knife manufacturing facility, and the opportunities presented by working as apprentices to a master sorcerer. McMurphy didn't know what the word "conglomerate" meant, but he had an instinctive grasp of the concept.

Bloody Bob didn't really have a head for business, but for a magic visor of his own, he would have sold his soul. His brawn came in very handy. While the others worked, Brewster supervised and drew up plans and concentrated on making a suitable pair of spectacles for Bob. It proved to be a bit more difficult than he'd expected.

He had never thought it would be easy. He understood the

principles involved, but he was not a trained optometrist and he had realized that this was not going to be one of those "get-your-glasses-in-one-hour" jobs. He had access to glass, because Mick kept a stock of crude glass blocks and pipettes in his laboratory, but he didn't have access to any modern grinders, and so he had to improvise.

It had been necessary for Mick to make two wheels, constructed to Brewster's specifications, one for grinding and one for polishing. They were essentially similar in design to potter's wheels, but grinding and polishing on them took forever. To grind the lenses, Brewster had to use fine sand and water from the stream, and to polish them he used hide and sheepskin. The result was hardly comparable to a modern pair of lenses, but in time, he was able to come up with something more or less serviceable, even if it did take a lot of elbow grease.

It was also, unavoidably, a trial-and-error process, most of it simply guesswork. He would make one pair of lenses, try them out on Bloody Bob, see how well they worked—or didn't work—and then go back to the drawing board. (Or, more properly, the grinding wheel.) There was also the problem of testing them. Initially, he had prepared an eye chart, handprinted on a board, only to discover that the letters meant nothing to Bloody Bob because he couldn't read. McMurphy came to the rescue, however, and drew another sort of eye chart.

Brewster would point to one large picture at the very top. "What's this, Bob?"

"Uh . . . 'tis a cow, Doc."

"Okay. Good. Now, let's move on to the next line, with these smaller pictures here. What animal is this?"

"Uh . . . a rabbit?"

"Good. Now how about this one?"

"A pig."

"Well, no, actually, this one's a sheep."

"Looks like a pig."

" 'Tis a sheep, Bob," McMurphy would put in.

"Still looks like a pig. You drew it wrong, McMurphy."

"You think a farmer can't tell the difference 'twixt a sheep and a pig?"

"I say 'tis a pig!" (Rasp of a new sword being drawn from its scabbard.)

"Okay, okay, 'tis a pig!"

"Uh, maybe we'd better try this again later," Brewster would say.

Eventually, he was able to make a pair of lenses that allowed Bloody Bob to see reasonably well, even if his vision was still a little blurry, but to Bloody Bob, this was a miracle. And the fact that it took so long obviously meant it was a very complicated thaumaturgic process, indeed.

Then there arose the problem of making frames for the lenses. Plastic, obviously, was out of the question, so they would have to be metal frames. And while metal frames could be fashioned without too much trouble, someone like Bloody Bob would require something pretty strong and durable. Wire rims simply wouldn't do. It was Bloody Bob himself who finally gave Brewster the solution to the problem. He had referred to Brewster's glasses as a "magic visor," so what Brewster came up with and had Mick make was, in fact, a sort of visor, made from two pieces constructed out of bronze and riveted together, between which the lenses could be sandwiched. In fact, the finished product bore a strong resemblance to the sort of wraparound glasses that were popular for a time among musicians and surfers.

Bloody Bob was ecstatic. Not only did they help him see better than he had in years, they were also a unique fashion statement that gave him an even more fearsome appearance. When he first put them on, he did so with as much reverence and solemnity as a king putting on his crown. From that moment on, Bloody Bob was Brewster's loyal friend and stalwart champion, which he declared formally by dropping to one knee and swearing his lifelong allegiance.

All this took time, however, and as the keep slowly started to shape up, there were other projects in the works, as well. Mick and McMurphy undertook the construction of the still, working under Brewster's supervision. They fashioned copper tubing by using iron rods from the smithy, wrapping copper sheets around them, then heating them and beating them into solid tubes, which they then pulled off the rods. Solder was made from a blend of tin and gold, which Brewster thought rather extravagant, but Mick dismissed his concerns by telling him that he had plenty of the stuff and it wasn't really worth anything, anyway.

This was yet one more tidbit of information that gave Brewster pause, for gold had always been valued throughout history and he could not think of a time when it had been considered essentially worthless. He did not know what to make of it. He watched as the molten blend of gold and tin was poured into a mold, so that it came out in the shape of a thin rod, and then all it took was an iron rod heated in the furnace to make a crude yet effective soldering iron. Slowly, but surely, what he thought had to be the most expensive still in history started to take shape.

Another project they devoted time to was the construction of a Franklin stove, to heat Brewster's new residence in the tower. Brewster drew up the plans and Mick fashioned a square box of iron plate, with a hole in the top and bricks inside it to hold the heat. Then they made a pipe to conduct the smoke out through the chimney of the fireplace, which worked just fine once they cleared out all the squirrels' nests.

The next project they began was the construction of a

cistern to be placed atop the tower. The plan was to run it off the large wooden water wheel by devising a set of three smaller wooden wheels, one of which was mounted on the outer wall beside the main water wheel, while the other two were mounted on the exterior wall of the tower, one at the bottom and one at the very top. These were all connected by a crude belt drive system made from rope and wooden pegs. The large, main water wheel turned the first smaller wooden wheel mounted beside it. This wheel was connected to the second smaller wheel by a horizontal belt, and that second wheel, in turn, was connected to the third wheel by a vertical belt that ran up to the top of the tower. Between the pegs of the vertical belt drive, wooden buckets had been mounted to lift water from the sluice to the cistern at the top of the tower, where a tipover allowed the buckets to automatically dump the water in a small wooden trough that filled the cistern. There was an overflow trough that allowed the excess water to drain back down to the sluice.

To improve this operation even further, Brewster had redesigned the sluice itself, so that instead of the gate being opened at the channel which diverted water from the stream to the bottom of the wheel, an elevated wooden sluice was constructed, starting a short distance upstream of the keep, which brought water to the top of the wheel—in principle, much like a Roman aqueduct. This allowed the main water wheel to turn faster and operate more efficiently.

The purpose of the cistern was to provide fresh drinking water for Brewster's residence and, he hoped, eventually a flush toilet. To this end, Brewster drew up plans for a septic tank and a leach field. The excavation would be located about thirty feet downstream of the keep.

All of these projects were somewhat labor intensive, and would certainly have been a lot of work for just four people. However, they had help. Each day, as work progressed, new volunteers were added to the labor force. The first had been Fuzzy Tom, who showed up the day after Bloody Bob to meet the new sorcerer and see this interesting construction project Bob had told him about.

Fuzzy Tom was one of the brigands, a retired warrior like Bloody Bob, with a rotund body and a thick mass of wavy, black hair that fell down to his shoulders. He had a large and bushy black beard that started at his cheekbones and grew down to his chest, so that all anyone could see of his face was a short expanse of forehead and two twinkling brown eyes. He possessed a rather pleasant, laid-back disposition that under any other circumstances would have prevented him from doing anything that even remotely resembled work. However, Mick explained that this was sorcery, not work, and Fuzzy Tom fell for it. He pitched right in, and when he came back the next day, he brought Froggy Bruce, Malicious Mike, and Pikestaff Pat.

Froggy Bruce was a quiet, soft-spoken brigand with long, fine, sandy-blond hair, a wispy beard, and large, sad-looking eyes that gave him something of the aspect of his namesake. He also happened to be very fond of frogs. Not eating them, collecting them. He owned dozens and dozens, all of which he kept in his room at the tavern in Brigand's Roost. He liked to entertain and his place, one might say, was always jumping.

Malicious Mike was a dark and brooding young man who always dressed in black and apologized politely whenever he crushed somebody's skull. He could not abide rudeness in a person and always said "please" and "thank you" whenever he robbed someone. Some people thought he was being maliciously sarcastic, hence his name, but the fact was that Mike simply believed in good manners, regardless of the circumstances.

Pikestaff Pat was almost as thin as his weapon of choice,

a long, slim pikestaff that he always carried with him on his shoulder. He had dark red hair and a neatly trimmed beard. What he lacked in size compared to the other brigands, he made up for with aggressive energy and a sharp wit. He was one of the few married brigands and he never went anywhere without a lunch wrapped in a kerchief and tied to his pikestaff by his wife, Calamity Jane, who relentlessly pursued the fruitless task of trying to put some meat on his bones.

Calamity herself showed up on the third day, partly because she was curious and partly because she wanted to make sure her husband had enough to eat. An intense, voluptuous, young woman with short dark hair and a perpetual squint, she arrived in a cart loaded with provisions for the boys. She stood up to wave at Pat and promptly executed a near-perfect half gainer off the cart, ending with a face-plant in the mud. Over the next few hours, she tripped over everything in sight, knocked over tables, fell from ladders, and took no less than three impromptu dips in the creek. She caused such consternation that Mick suggested she stop trying to help with the construction and concentrate on cooking for the hungry crew, which effort she took up with enthusiasm. She only scalded herself six times.

As word of what Brewster was doing began to spread, more people showed up to see these wonders for themselves and wound up volunteering for the project. It was like an old-time frontier house-raising. Everyone pitched in until there were over forty people bustling about, which constituted almost the entire population of Brigand's Roost and all the surrounding farms. Mick assigned tasks to everyone, so that some people worked only on the still, while others built the elevated sluice, the cistern, the wheels, and the belt drive for the water lift, and so on. Each of them took great pride in what they were doing, and set to with enthusiasm, for it was both an opportunity to help get a sorcerer settled in their neighborhood and participate in important magical works.

The grounds of the keep soon had awnings erected on them, beneath which the labor force could rest during their breaks, and the brush and tall grass were soon trampled down by all the activity. Small pits were dug for cookfires, and as night fell and work ceased, the kettles were removed and logs were added, making for cheery campfires around which people gathered to tell stories and sing songs.

Storytelling, Brewster soon discovered, was by far the most popular form of entertainment, and most of these stories were built around the actual experiences and exploits of the storyteller, usually embellished considerably for dramatic effect. There were also legends, which were stories that had been passed down through the generations, and made for a kind of historical record, though not a very reliable one, as each individual storyteller usually added something to the tale.

Brewster's presence at these campfire tales was especially appreciated, as most sorcerers had a tendency to hold themselves aloof from the common throng and avoided socializing with the general populace. Each storyteller tried to top the others for his benefit, and the audience was nothing if not critical. Each tale was followed by a chorus of "Well told! Well told!" or "Bah, I've heard it better!" or "Nay, you forgot the part about the virgin!"

Brewster heard "The Tale of Frank the Usurper and How the Kingdom Got Its Name," an abbreviated version of which he'd already heard from Mick; "The Tale of the Undeflowered Whore," which was apparently a very popular one; "The Life and Times of Bloody Bob," told haltingly by Bloody Bob himself, in which most recalled encounters ended with the phrase "And then I smote him good!"

and "The Lament of Handsome Hal," who was driven mad by a nymph who fell in love with him, a story Brewster thought was a marvelously witty fairy tale, never suspecting for a moment that it had really happened, which it had.

"Pat, tell the tale of The Werepot Prince," said Calamity, nudging her husband sharply in the ribs with her elbow.

"Jane, they've all heard it a dozen times or more," protested Pikestaff Pat.

"Perhaps Doc hasn't," Calamity replied. "And anyway, I like the way you tell it."

"Yes, I'd like to hear it," Brewster said.

"Mike tells it better," Pikestaff Pat replied.

"Nay, go on, you tell it, Pat," Malicious Mike insisted.

And after a bit more coaxing, Pikestaff Pat stood and embarked upon his tale.

" 'Tis 'The Tale of the Werepot Prince,' " he began, "and they say it happened hereabouts, a long, long time ago. Perhaps"—he paused significantly and glanced around—"at this very place where we are gathered on this night."

There was a collective "Oooh!" and someone remarked, "Nice touch, very nice touch, indeed."

"The prince I speak of was a handsome, bold, and strapping young chap name of Brian," Pat continued, "sole heir to his father's throne. Now, bein' an only child, Brian was a wee bit spoiled by his folks and allowed to have his way in most things. If he wanted to have himself a brand-new puppy, why 'twasn't good enough that he had one, but he was given three. If he wasn't up to finishin' all the veggies on his plate, why no one made him do so, never mind that kids was starvin' off in India."

"India?" said Brewster.

"Aye, well, no one knows quite where this Kingdom of India was, y'see, and ain't no one anybody knows what's ever been there, but 'twas gen'ral knowledge that kids was always starvin' there,'' said Pat.

"I see," said Brewster with a puzzled frown.

"Anyways," continued Pat, "Prince Brian ain't never had to do no chores around the palace, never had to mow the lawn or clean his room, nor even make his bed. Had servants for all that sort of thing, y'know, provided by his mum, the queen. And he never said 'please' nor 'thank you,' neither," Pat added with a glance at Malicious Mike, who nodded in acknowledgement that he hadn't left that important part of the story out.

"Prince Brian the Bold was his proper, officially sanctioned appellation," Pat continued, "but to most folks in the kingdom, he was merely Brian the Brat, and a bit of a royal pain, to boot. The young girls of the kingdom loved him dearly, they did, for he was comely to look upon, what with his curly golden locks and pleasin' form, and word had it he was right properly endowed, as well, though 'twas only hearsay, mind. Y'know how young girls talk.

"Many's the time our Brian hopped a fence and had himself a lovely moonlight interlude with some fair young village maid, but he was never caught, y'see, so either he was very much adroit or else the lad was blamed for every other swollen belly in the kingdom, like as not to protect a boyfriend who wasn't royalty, y'see, and therefore not immune to parental retribution. But either way, by the time our lad was some twenty summers old, there was more lovely little gold-haired rug rats in the kingdom than you could shake a stick at, and a surprisin' number of them was named Brian, too.

"Yet one day, there came a time when our Prince Brian cast his wanderin' orbs in a somewhat unfortunate direction. Unfortunate for him, as 'twould turn out. He got himself right bent out of shape over a young maid name of Katherine, who was as pretty a wench as you could ever hope to see. Fifteen summers old, she was, a ripe bloomin' young thing, with big blue eyes and lovely bosoms and a saucy look about her what made you want to throw her down and mount the pony. Leastwise, she had that effect on Brian, whom she discommoded somethin' awful.

"Now Brian, used to havin' his own way, went and set his cap at her, and some other parts what were located lower down, as well. He started sendin' her love notes and flowers and the like, which gifts the wench did not refuse, but she went and showed 'em to her father, which was when the trouble started.

"Saucy Katherine's father, as it turns out, was the local sorcerer, a fearsome wizard name of Catrack or Hatrack or some such thing—"

"'Twas Catrack," Malicious Mike said.

"Nay, 'twas Hatrack," Fuzzy Tom disputed.

"'Twasn't neither, 'twas Carnac," someone else called out, and a loud and vociferous argument ensued, which ended abruptly when Pikestaff Pat put two fingers in his mouth and whistled loudly and piercingly.

"*As I was sayin'*," he continued, "there seems to have been some dispute as to his name, but whatever in bloody hell his name was, he wasn't pleased with this attention bein' royally bestowed on his one and only child. He went to the king and said, 'Now listen here, Your Majesty, boys will be boys and all that sort of thing, but I'd kindly appreciate your tellin' your young whelp to keep his royal, horny little mitts to his own self, if it please Your Majesty. I'd sorta had my heart set on Katherine marryin' an adept and keepin' to the family tradition and all that sort of thing, and while I've nothin' against royalty, y'understand, I'd just as soon she not go marryin' beneath her station, if 'tis all the same to you.'

"Now, such remarks ain't gen'rally considered proper protocol when speakin' to your basic monarch," Pat explained, "but be that as it may, the king had no choice but to swallow it, or else risk bein' turned into a toadstool or havin' himself struck with a spell what makes his loins go dry, and so he grinned and bore it and nodded that he understood and told the wizard, 'Aye, indeed, I quite see what you mean. I'll have a word with my young royal son and see to it that it won't go happenin' again.' Whereupon the wizard left and His Majesty the King turned to Her Majesty the Queen and said, 'Go tell Brian to leave young Katherine alone or he's liable to cock everything up.' "

A collective groan went up around the campfire.

"Well," said Pat, as he resumed the tale, "the queen spoke to Prince Brian about young Katherine, but young blood runnin' hot and all that, our lad was not dissuaded. He pursued his suit, and one night after Katherine's dad set out for a meetin' of the Guild, he pressed it home. Her father was not expected back for quite some time, y'see, as the journey would have taken many days and then there was the meetin', what with banquets and speech-makin' and activities and all, and then the journey back, so Katherine and Brian made the most of Daddy's absence and frolicked with great vigor every night he was away.

"The trouble came much later, after Katherine's dad came home. One day, he noticed that his daughter was puttin' on a little weight, y'see, and then she started feelin' sickly in the mornin', and fairly soon it all came clear that Katherine was carryin' a child. She confessed all to her father, who flew into a frothin' rage and retired to his wizard's chambers, from whence he did not emerge for many days and nights."

Pat paused for dramatic effect, looking around at his audience, who waited eagerly for the tale to resume.

"In the meantime," he continued after a moment, "Prince Brian was hangin' about the palace with his falcons and his hounds, dashin' off on huntin' expeditions and carousin' with his mates, little suspectin' that he was about to be a father . . . nor that Hatrack—"

"Catrack," Malicious Mike corrected him.

"*Katherine's dad*," said Pat pointedly, "was gatherin' his powers to cast a nasty evil curse, a spell most horrible and frightful. The way he saw it, his daughter had been spoiled, her honor and her dignity besmirched, and nothin' would do but for Prince Brian to suffer the same fate. So, in the darkness of his wizard's chambers, the sorcerer conjured up a spell, usin' a lock of hair that Brian had carelessly given to Katherine as a keepsake.

"And as the legend has it, one day, the servants came to tidy up Prince Brian's room and make his bed, and what they found betwixt the sheets, and not beneath the bed, where such contrivances are usually kept, was a bright and shiny golden chamberpot, embellished with some emeralds and rubies, much like the ones that Brian always wore on a chain around his neck."

He paused again and looked around, nodding significantly.

"Well, need it be said, there was no sign of Brian, and though the king sent men to search throughout the land, no trace of him was ever found. The chamberpot, 'twas said, had disappeared as well, stolen by a servant who thought to prise the jewels from it and sell 'em, but when he tried, lo and behold, the chamberpot cried out! The frightened servant left well enough alone and sold it to the first trader he came across, and what became of it after that is anybody's guess.

"However, legend has it that when the moon is full, Prince Brian walks again as his normal self, such bein' the nature of the curse, so that he can always remember how it feels to be human, a cruel and brief reminder to torment him when he turns back into a receptacle for human waste, which is what Katherine's father considered him to be, and had thus condemned him for eternity. So if you should ever find yourself in some strange hostelry or tavern, take care if you should feel the call of nature in the middle of the night, especially if the moon be full. For should you reach down underneath your bed and happen to pull a golden chamberpot with gems set in it, have a care . . . for you never know, it just might turn out to be a royal pain in the arse."

"Well told! Well told!"

"Bah, I've heard it better."

"Nay, I liked the bit about the starvin' kids in India. And the frolickin' with vigor, 'twas a nice touch."

And so it went, with critical appraisals being exchanged and argued back and forth, until the evening started to grow cold and they all retired to the great hall in Brewster's keep. They built a big fire in the hearth and Mick broke open a fresh cash of peregrine wine. Torches were lit and placed up in the wall sconces. Brewster sat in the honored place at the table on the dais, with Mick on his right and Bloody Bob on his left, while all the other brigands and a few of the farmers in the crowd packed the other tables, drinking heartily and laughing boisterously, pounding each other on the back and looking very much like a scene from an Errol Flynn movie.

And what of poor Pamela, waiting patiently in London for her fiancé to return? Well, Brewster had not forgotten about Pamela and was concerned that she might be worried about him, but under his current circumstances, there was really nothing he could do. He was stuck until he could locate the missing time machine, and though he had salvaged what he could from the one that had exploded, intending to use some of the parts for his project in the keep, there was no hope whatsoever of rebuilding it. The best he could do was to make himself as comfortable as possible in his new and unfamiliar surroundings, and hope that word would spread about the missing time machine and that someone would turn up some information.

Mick had announced to everyone that Brewster Doc had lost a magic chariot and then Brewster gave them all a brief description of it, asking that if anyone should see or hear about such a device, they should immediately let him know. However, no one had stepped forward, though they all promised to keep their eyes and ears open.

All of them except three of the younger brigands, that is—Long Bill, Fifer Bob, and Silent Fred, who looked at each other nervously when Brewster described the appearance of the missing time machine. However, Brewster didn't notice this, nor did anybody else. (Nor will the narrator explain at this point why they did not step forward, for they obviously knew something. This is a technique of storytelling known as foreshadowing and all will be made clear at the proper time. Don't worry, remember, always trust the narrator.)

Anyway, where were we? Oh, right, we're in the middle of this rowdy, boisterous banquet scene in the great hall, with Brewster sitting in the place of honor at the table on the dais, Mick on his right, Bloody Bob on his left, torches flickering, fire burning in the hearth, peregrine wine flowing, food being thrown, and a good time generally being had by all . . . but wait. What's this? The sound of hoofbeats rapidly approaching, unheard by the revelers because they're making so much noise. Unheard, that is, until the horse and rider came bursting into the great hall with a noisy clattering of hooves on the stone floor.

A table overturned, and people scattered, and the handsome, jet-black stallion reared up dramatically and neighed as it was reined in by the black-clad rider in the center of the hall.

Silence descended like an anvil...only much softer. Silence that was not broken by a single whisper or a murmur, save for a very quiet "Uh-oh" from Bloody Bob.

The black-clad rider dismounted and dropped the reins, and the stallion obediently remained standing still as the rider took several steps forward and stopped in the exact center of the room, sweeping it with her smoldering gaze as she stood, legs braced wide apart, one hand on the dagger in her belt, the other on her sword hilt.

"What the devil's going on here?"

"Who is *that?*" Brewster asked with awe.

"That," Mick replied in a soft voice, "is none other than Black Shannon."

CHAPTER
<u>SIX</u>

Some entrance, huh? The funny thing is, Shannon did not think of it that way at all. Which is not to say she lacked a sense of drama. Under most circumstances, she was very good at thinking things out in advance, which was one of the reasons she was the leader of the brigands. She knew how to plan a job, and she often planned them quite dramatically, indeed. However, when she lost her temper (and it didn't take much), it was like a case of spontaneous combustion. She rode her horse into the great hall of the keep not so much for effect, but because it was the quickest way to get there. She had never been one to waste much time, especially when she was angry.

She had been away, casing a few jobs and doing a little cruising on the side. She often did this sort of thing. She would leave her trademark, black leather, lace-up jerkin, and matching, skintight, leather breeches and high boots, in Brigand's Roost, then ride off to some town or village, looking quite demure in a long, sweeping peasant skirt and low-cut blouse, with dainty little slippers on her feet. Once there, she would circulate and keep her eyes and ears open, on the lookout for any gossip about trade shipments and the like.

Often, she would take a job for a few days, working in a local tavern, where one could hear all sorts of things. With her stunning looks, she never had any trouble getting hired or getting men to talk about their business, the better to impress her. While she struck up conversations and remained on the lookout for income-producing opportunities, she kept a lookout for possible romantic opportunities, as well.

To say that Shannon was beautiful would be an understatement. Ordinary adjectives simply wouldn't do her justice, only superlatives sufficed. She stood five feet seven inches tall and was perfectly proportioned, with the kind of body that could only be described as luscious. Her face was breathtakingly lovely and deceptively angelic. She had pale, creamy skin and blue eyes that were so bright, they almost seemed to glow. All the usual clichés applied—lips just made for kissing, raven tresses that simply begged to be caressed, etc., etc.—only more so. However, these were only her most obvious and superficial attributes.

What most men failed to note was that she was astonishingly fit. Her arms were slender, but they were firm and hard, and if she were to flex, disconcertingly developed biceps would stand out. Her shoulders were lovely, but they were also broad and well defined. And if her waist did not betray an ounce of fat, it was because she had stomach muscles like a washboard. The way she held herself, and the catlike way she moved, revealed to the observant eye that this was no ordinary peasant girl, but a young woman who had trained long and hard, and *not* at waiting tables.

What most men also failed to see (because they were too busy looking elsewhere) was that behind those coyly fluttering eyelashes, her eyes were not only blue enough to get lost in, but alert, direct, and penetrating in their gaze. Men also never noticed now easily she led them into talking about themselves, about their business, their plans, their personal lives, their foibles, and how much money they had. They were so busy trying to impress and flatter her that they were never aware of being cleverly manipulated.

Men, however, have always had a tendency to see that which they want to see in women, and then to act, often compulsively, on their impressions. This was something Shannon learned while she was still quite young, and she had also learned how to take advantage of it. Men, so far as she was concerned, were really only good for two things— sex and lifting heavy objects. Beyond that, she didn't have much use for them. However, as Shannon saw it, just because men were rather limited in their uses was no reason not to use them. At least once.

Shannon had started early and learned quickly. At the age of thirteen, she had been seduced by the handsome, eighteen-year-old son of a very wealthy merchant. Within about six weeks, that merchant gradually lost a significant proportion of his inventory. Shannon sold the goods her ardent swain had stolen from his father and turned a tidy profit in the bargain. The profits, she had told the merchant's son, would be used to start a brand-new life. She somehow neglected to mention that this new life did not include him.

Thus Shannon had embarked upon an ever-escalating life of crime. At one time or another, she had been called an evil bitch, a soulless heartbreaker, an accomplished liar, a crafty thief, a merciless killer, and an amoral slut (which raises the question of what a moral slut would be, and the answer is, of course, an honest one). Though Shannon would have reacted quickly and decisively had anyone the foolishness to call her any of those things to her face, privately she would admit to all of them, for she was not given to hypocrisy. Men had taught her what she knew and she merely paid them back in kind. She was not, she often told herself, completely without scruples. If a man came along who treated her with civility and honesty, she would treat him likewise. However, she had learned that such men were in very rare supply.

Not even the brigands whom she led knew much about her history, though by the time her path crossed theirs, she had already developed quite a reputation. She was known to be a swordswoman of extraordinary skill, and when she first took up with the brigands, a few of them had this confirmed for them the hard way. This gave her no small measure of respect. By virtue of her abilities and her intelligence, she soon became their leader and they prospered under her direction.

Though Shannon was a woman of lusty and, some might say, rather excessive appetites, she had always avoided romantic entanglements with any of the brigands. She knew that it would only complicate things. She had an instinctive grasp of the fact that excessive fraternalization does not make for good leadership. Aside from that, she did not find any of the brigands especially attractive. Most of them were great, big, hairy louts who rarely washed—though she insisted they bathe in the creek whenever the stench became too rank. In general, Shannon preferred to indulge her lusty appetitites on her frequent scouting expeditions, or by abducting the occasional handsome male traveler encountered during one of their holdups.

She was never recognized, because whenever the brigands plied their trade, she always wore a mask consisting of a large black bandanna with two eyeholes cut in it, which covered her entire face except her mouth and chin. In imitation of her, the other brigands wore black masks as well, which led to their becoming known as the Black

Brigands, which they thought had a very nice ring to it, indeed.

Most of the local citizenry knew what Shannon looked like without her mask, but she had nothing to fear from them. The bandits never robbed the locals and Shannon never hesitated to provide assistance if local citizens were in need of help. She never asked for any compensation in return. This, she reasoned quite correctly, was merely good public relations. The result was that every time one of the king's patrols came to Brigand's Roost, there was not a brigand to be found and no matter whom they asked, the replies were always the same.

"Brigands? What brigands? We've never been troubled by brigands around here. Actually, we only changed the name from Turkey's Roost to attract tourism."

Which brings us back to Shannon's angry and dramatic entrance, just in case you thought your narrator got sidetracked. When she returned from one of her scouting expeditions, much like king's patrols, she found the town almost completely empty, except for a few old people who were habitually cranky and never felt like going anywhere. From them, she'd learned that everyone had gone off to a revel at Mick O'Fallon's mill. They didn't bother telling her about the sorcerer who'd recently arrived, because the oldsters were rather crotchety and rather liked the thought of getting the young folks into hot water.

Shannon did not take kindly to this news. She had gone to all the trouble of setting up a system to be followed in her absence, whereby the brigands would work in shifts, lurking by the forest trails, waylaying coaches and unwary travelers, and instead of following instructions, they were goofing off. She paused only long enough to change before galloping off to kick some brigand butt. As she rode, she grew angrier and angrier, and as she approached the keep and heard the sounds of revelry, she became absolutely furious.

Had she paused to think, she would have realized that there was something unusual about this situation. For one thing, Mick O'Fallon was not known to be especially gregarious. For Mick to hold a revel was decidedly out of character, and it was unlikely that he would allow anyone else to hold a revel at his mill. Furthermore, just about everyone in Brigand's Roost had gone, including One-Eyed Jack, the tavern keeper, who never left his place of business, and Dirty Mary with her fancy girls, who were actually rather plain, and even the Awful Urchin Gang, a band of grubby little children whose awfulness was measured by the fact that all their parents insisted they were orphans. And no one, least of all Mick, would ever consider inviting *them* anywhere.

Shannon had not paused to consider any of these things, however, and as she approached the keep, all she could think of was that the brigands were Absent Without Leave, and for that, heads were going to roll. Or at the very least get generously thumped. She kicked her horse and went charging up to the front door.

Rascal Rick had chosen that unfortunate moment to go answer the call of nature. As he opened the door, he saw the fearsome apparition of Shannon mounted on her black stallion, Big Nasty, bearing down on him. He froze in his tracks and was knocked ass over teakettle as she rode right over him and galloped straight into the hall.

She dismounted and angrily demanded to know what in hell was going on. When a reply was not immediately forthcoming, she grabbed the nearest brigand by the hair and violently yanked him backward off the bench, onto the floor.

"*Explain yourself!*" she demanded.

Unfortunately, the brigand she had grabbed was Silent Fred, who spoke only about once or twice a year. No one could recall him ever actually speaking an entire sentence in a conversation.

"Well. . . ." said Fred, and shrugged elaborately, which was quite a speech for him, all things considered.

Shannon grunted with disdain and kicked him aside, then gave him another kick in the rump for good measure as he scuttled away. She seized the next nearest victim by the ear. This misfortune fell to Froggy Bruce.

"*What is the meaning of this?*" she demanded, twisting his ear painfully. "*Who gave you miserable curs leave to depart the Roost?*"

"Well, actually," said Froggy Bruce, speaking in a calm and level tone of voice, despite the painful grip she had on him, "there's a perfectly reasonable explanation for all this. You see, the fact of the matter is that . . ."

She walloped him across his head, which made his eyes bulge out even more than they normally did. The sound of the blow echoed in the hall and made everyone who heard it wince.

"Ow," said Froggy Bruce with characteristic understatement.

Shannon's hand flashed to her sword hilt and the blade sang free of its scabbard, whistled through the air, and came down on the table, passing uncomfortably close to Long Bill's left ear and splitting an entire roast turkey in half.

"*Who watches the trails?*" she demanded furiously. "*Who lurks in the hedgerows? Who waylays unsuspecting travelers? Am I expected to do all the work around here? Am I to bear all the burden of responsibility? Do you think money grows on trees?*"

Brewster stood and cleared his throat politely. "Uh . . . excuse me, Miss Shannon?"

Shannon turned and, for the first time, noticed his unfamiliar presence.

"I'm afraid I'm the one who's responsible for all this," he said. "I'm sorry, I truly didn't realize that it would cause a problem. I hope you won't hold that against me."

"And who might *you* be?" she asked with a frown.

"Uh, this is Brewster Doc," said Bloody Bob helpfully, getting up to perform the formal introductions. "He's—"

"Did I ask *you*, you great oaf?" Shannon interrupted brusquely.

"Uh . . . no . . ."

"Then sit down and be silent! Let the man speak for himself," she snapped.

With a sheepish grimace, Bloody Bob meekly resumed his seat.

"Brewster Doc, eh?" Shannon said, approaching so she could look him over.

"Well, most of my friends just call me Doc," said Brewster with a smile.

" 'Tis early yet to presume friendship," Shannon replied. The entire hall was silent, every eye upon them.

"Well, yes, I suppose I see your point," said Brewster. "However, I'm very pleased to meet you, just the same." He held out his hand.

She stared at him thoughtfully for a moment, then sheathed her sword and clasped his forearm.

"I am called Shannon," she said.

"You have a strong grip," said Brewster.

"For a wench, you mean?" she said sarcastically.

"For anyone," said Brewster with a shrug.

She looked him over appraisingly. " 'Tis strange garb you wear. You have not the aspect of a native of these parts."

"Well, actually, I came from London," Brewster said.

"Lun-dun?" She looked puzzled. "I know of no such place."

" 'Tis in the far distant Land of Ing," said Mick, "in another place and time."

"Another place and time?" said Shannon, glancing at him sharply. "What do you mean?"

" 'Tis a mighty sorcerer, he is," said Mick. "His magic chariot fell from the sky."

"Are you drunk?" she asked him.

Mick drew himself up with affronted dignity. "We little people do not get drunk," he said with an air of wounded pride. "We merely grow loquacious."

"Babbling nonsense by any other name is still babbling nonsense," Shannon replied. "I have never heard of wizards who could fly."

"Faith, and I was there, wasn't I?" said Mick. "I *saw* it, I tell you. 'Tis a place of mighty sorcerers, this Land of Ing. People fly there all the time in magic chariots. 'Tis such a commonplace occurrence, they do not even call 'em *magic* chariots; they call 'em *plains*. He told me so himself."

"And you say you *saw* this magic chariot fall from the sky with your own eyes?" said Shannon dubiously, glancing from Mick to Brewster, then back to Mick again.

"Aye, that I did, and didn't it almost crush me when it fell?" said Mick.

"Where is this chariot now?" asked Shannon, still not entirely convinced.

" 'Twas broken in the fall," said Mick. "And then McMurphy's foolish bull attacked it, and Doc had no choice but to blast it with a bolt of thunder."

"Aye, 'tis true," McMurphy added. " 'Twas nothing left of it but bits of roasted meat scattered about."

"Hmmm," said Shannon, pursing her lips thoughtfully and staring at Brewster with new interest.

He certainly did not look like a mighty sorcerer, she thought. He dressed strangely, but there was nothing noble or fearsome about his appearance. She knew that most sorcerers took great pains to look noble or fearsome, preferably both at the same time, and if they couldn't manage that, they at least sought to look striking. This one did not even look striking. He looked rather rumpled, and there was something about him that brought to mind a little boy. A lost little boy. She decided to find out more about this sorcerer.

"Leave us," she said to the others. "All of you, back to the Roost! And, you farmers, back to your turnips and your milk cows! I would speak more with this sorcerer, alone."

Some of the brigands exchanged nervous looks and Dirty Mary's fancy girls hid smug little smiles behind their hands, but no one questioned Shannon's orders. They all left, with much scraping of benches and shuffling of feet and clinking of swords and other accoutrements, until only McMurphy, Mick, and Bloody Bob were left with Shannon and Brewster in the hall.

She raised her eyebrows. "Well?" she said.

"You mean us, too?" McMurphy asked innocently.

"I said that I would speak with the sorcerer alone, did I not?" she said, a dangerous edge to her voice.

"But Mick and I are his apprentices," protested McMurphy unwisely.

"Uh . . . and I am his loyal retainer," Bloody Bob added.

"Retainer, eh?" said Shannon. "Well, if 'tis your teeth you'll be retaining, then you'll do as you're bloody well told, you great ox. As for you 'apprentices' . . ."

"We're going, we're going," McMurphy said hastily.

Mick glanced uneasily at Brewster.

"So long as you would not object, of course," said Shannon, her voice dripping with irony as she turned to

Brewster. "Far be it from me to order your apprentices about," she added with a nice dollop of sarcasm.

"Oh, no, I have no objection," Brewster said.

"How nice," she said wryly. "My thanks for your indulgence." She gave him a little mock bow and then turned to the others. "*Out!*"

With uneasy glances at Brewster, they departed without another word, leaving him alone with Shannon.

"So," she said, coming around the table and stepping up onto the dais, "now we may become properly acquainted."

She came closer, gazing at Brewster with an intense, predatory look.

"You shall be my first adept," she said. "And I do hope you are. Adept, that is."

"I beg your pardon?" Brewster said.

"Of course, if you really are a wizard, you could strike me with a spell," she continued, drawing nearer. "Or perhaps a thunderbolt. You could have me completely at your mercy."

She reached out and grasped the lapels of his jacket with both hands, then abruptly pulled him toward her and gave him a kiss that would have weakened the resolution of a priest. (Some priests, of course, have more resolve than others, but this is merely a figure of speech. Suffice it to say that Shannon's skill at kissing was exceeded only by her willfulness.)

Brewster's eyes were wide with astonishment as Shannon broke off the kiss, smiled, and said, "You see, I also know how to cast a spell."

She unsheathed her sword and swept off the surface of the table with the blade, sending goblets, meats, and fruit baskets crashing to the floor. Then she tossed her sword aside, swung him down onto his back on the tabletop, sat astride him, and ripped open his shirt.

Now, it is a recognized fact of life that most men are intimidated by self-confident, aggressive women. This is because men, generally speaking, like to feel that they are in control. And most women know that so long as a man *thinks* that he is control, he's not too difficult to manage. Shannon understood this very well. She was an expert at making men think they were in control, when she was actually controlling them quite subtly. However, when she chose to, she could also take control directly and there was nothing subtle about it whatsoever. She knew that both approaches had their uses.

If Brewster was, indeed, as powerful a sorcerer as the others claimed, then he represented a potential threat. She had seen how quickly he had upset her system and had everyone in Brigand's Roost and the surrounding farms at his beck and call. Mick, who was hardly the gregarious sort, had a fascination for the thaumaturgic arts and if he was going to be this sorcerer's apprentice, then he would have less time for making arms and brewing wine, which were both commodities the brigands needed. McMurphy and the other farmers would have less time to tend their fields and provide the Roost with produce. Bloody Bob had even sworn allegiance to this sorcerer as his retainer, as if he were a king or something, and the other brigands had actually been *working* here, performing physical labor, which was unheard of. She'd seen the signs of it when she rode up to the keep. Her brigands, *working?* Nay, she thought, this wouldn't do at all. This was clearly a threat to her leadership and one that needed to be dealt with quickly and decisively.

She knew that taking on a sorcerer entailed a certain amount of risk; however, this sorcerer was nevertheless a man and men were all pushovers. The thing to do was take control of this situation in no uncertain terms, and do it quickly. She was confident of her abilities to arouse passion in a man and she knew that if she took the initiative in a firm, aggressive, brook-no-nonsense manner, she would quickly gain the upper hand.

The more important a man was, she'd learned, and the more power he wielded, the more susceptible he was to being dominated. Especially by a woman. Deep down inside, it was what they really wanted—to have the pins knocked out from under them by a strong, maternal figure who would tell them what to do. In her own uneducated way, Shannon was quite the student of human behavior, particularly male behavior, and she felt confident that this was the proper course to take. Besides, the guy was kinda cute.

"Uh . . . excuse me," Brewster said as she started to undo his belt, "but I think you have the wrong idea. You see, I happen to be engaged."

"Engaged in what?" she asked, momentarily thrown off her stride by the zipper and the little metal hook on the waistband of his gray flannel trousers. She frowned with puzzlement, uncertain how to proceed.

"Engaged to be married," replied Brewster.

"Oh," said Shannon, plucking at his waistband uncertainly. "You mean you are betrothed? What matters that to me?"

"Well, it matters to *me*," said Brewster. "And I expect it matters to Pamela, as well."

"Pamela? Is that the name of your intended?" The hook on the waistband popped free and Shannon uttered a satisfied "Ah! I see."

"It's not that I don't find you attractive, you understand," said Brewster, looking up at her, "it's just that I love Pamela, you see, and, well . . . I guess I'm a bit old-fashioned when it comes to this sort of thing. Besides, we hardly even know each other."

Shannon had finally figured out the zipper. She pulled it down, and her face lit up with a childlike delight.

"Oh! How clever!"

She pulled it back up again, then down, then up, then down and up, repeatedly, like a kid with a new toy.

"I mean, you said so yourself," continued Brewster, over the sounds of zipping, " 'tis a bit early to presume friendship, isn't it?"

"What?" said Shannon, looking up from his trousers to his face.

"I said . . ."

"I heard what you said," she replied irritably. Somehow, this wasn't going according to plan. "Who said anything about friendship?"

"Well . . ." Brewster hesitated awkwardly. "I mean, that *is* my zipper you're playing with, isn't it?"

"Zipper?" said Shannon. She zipped it up and down a couple of times. "Oh! I see. It *does* make a sort of zipping noise, doesn't it?"

"Yes, well, ripping open someone's shirt and unfastening their trousers does presume a certain degree of intimacy, doesn't it?" said Brewster.

Shannon frowned. She wasn't used to being distracted like this. Or to men being recalcitrant in such a situation. "Intimacy?" she said, raising her eyebrows. "What has this to do with intimacy? You're being ravished, you fool!"

"Oh," said Brewster. He cleared his throat. "I see. Well, if it's all the same to you, I'd really rather not be ravished right now, if you don't mind."

"You wouldn't?"

"No, I wouldn't," Brewster said. "I mean, don't get me wrong, I'm sure you're very good at it, but I'd really rather not."

"*S'trewth!*" said Shannon. "I've never heard of such a

thing. I'll have you know that most men would go quite out of their way to have me ravish them!"

"Oh, I'm sure of that," said Brewster, "and my reluctance is no reflection on you whatsoever. It's just that I happen to be spoken for and I think commitments are important, don't you?"

Shannon sighed. "Well . . . I suppose."

"This doesn't mean we can't be friends," said Brewster.

She put her hands on her hips and stared down at him with interest. "You are a most uncommon sort of man," she said. "Your Pamela must be quite a woman."

"Well, so are you," said Brewster diplomatically. "Actually, in some ways, the two of you would probably have much in common."

"Would we, indeed?" said Shannon with surprise. "Is she an outlaw, too?"

"No," admitted Brewster, "but she can be rather unconventional. She's also intelligent and very self-assured. Of course, she doesn't carry a sword, but she does look good in leather."

"Hmm," said Shannon, sitting back on Brewster's legs. She gazed down at him thoughtfully. "Is she . . . more beautiful than I?"

"Well, I don't know that I'd say that, exactly," Brewster replied. "I suppose you and she are beautiful in different ways, neither more than the other, merely different."

"Is her form more pleasing to you?"

"Uh . . . no, I wouldn't say that," Brewster replied awkwardly. He was unaccustomed to such frank discussions of comparative female anatomy, especially when such an incomparable piece of female anatomy was sitting right on top of him. "Actually, I've never really thought about it."

Shannon raised her eyebrows at this. A man who never really thought about a woman's body? This was a first.

Perhaps sorcerers really were different. "She is clever, then?"

"Well, yes," said Brewster. "She's very educated. She has doctorates in electrical engineering, mathematics, and computer science. She specializes in cybernetics."

Shannon frowned. She had no idea what those words meant, but they certainly sounded impressive. And then understanding seemed to dawn.

"Ah! She must be a sorceress!"

"Uh . . . well . . . uh . . ." Brewster shrugged. "Yeah, what the hell. She's a sorceress."

Shannon nodded, apparently satisfied with this explanation. "That makes a great difference, then," she said. " 'Tis your devotion to the magic arts which binds you. This I can understand."

"Good," said Brewster with relief. "Uh . . . do you think you could let me up now?"

"Oh, aye, of course," said Shannon, getting off him.

Brewster sat up, feeling very much relieved. "You've torn all the buttons off my shirt," he said, looking down at his exposed chest. And then he stood and exposed something else as his trousers fell down around his ankles.

Shannon's eyes grew wide. "*S'trewth!*" she exclaimed. "Never have I seen the like of *this!*"

"Umm . . . they're called boxer shorts," said Brewster with embarrassment as he hastily pulled up his trousers.

"What is their purpose?" Shannon asked in a puzzled tone.

"Uh . . . well . . ." Brewster hesitated. He had never been asked such a question before and it suddenly occurred to him that he had absolutely no idea. "They . . . uh . . . they . . . er . . . it has to do with magic. It would be too complicated to explain."

"And the significance of the little red lips?" Shannon asked.

"Uh . . ." Brewster blushed, cursing the day Pamela had bought the shorts for him. She had thought they were cute and liked to see him wearing them. "Well . . . uh . . . it has to do with a spell, you see."

Shannon frowned, and then her look of puzzlement changed to a knowing expression and a sly smile. "Oh! I see. 'Tis a spell of potency. Perhaps I was too hasty in letting you up."

"You're not going to—" Brewster began, alarmed, but Shannon chuckled and shook her head.

"Never fear, Wizard," she said. "I shall respect your pledge of troth, for in truth, you are the first man I have met who is true to his troth."

"I beg your pardon?" Brewster said. "Could you repeat that?"

Shannon shook her head. "I think not. It tangles the tongue. However, you are safe from me, for the sake of the beauteous sorceress Pamela. But never let it be said that a comely man escaped unravished from Black Shannon."

"I won't say anything about it," Brewster assured her. "As far as I'm concerned, nothing happened. All we did was talk."

"Nay!" said Shannon. "I said, never let it be said that a comely man escaped unravished from Black Shannon and I meant it, by the gods! I have a reputation to uphold, you know!"

"Oh," said Brewster. "Well . . . gee, I don't think I'd feel right saying that you'd ravished me."

"Then say nothing," Shannon replied. "None shall dare ask. You are a mighty wizard, after all, and I am Black Shannon. Let them think what they will."

Brewster cleared his throat. "Yes, well, I don't suppose we can do anything about what people choose to think."

"Indeed,"' said Shannon. "We shall be friends, then."

She held out her hand and they clasped each other's forearms.

"Friends," said Brewster with a nervous smile.

"But see here," Shannon said, "you have placed me in something of a quandary."

"I have?" said Brewster.

"Aye, you have, indeed," she replied. "You have all my brigands working here upon your . . . your works. True, 'tis a great boon to have a sorcerer settled in these parts, but my brigands have their outlaw trade to ply, you know. I cannot have them *working!* They will have no time left to steal and plunder! You see my difficulty, do you not?"

"Mmmm, yes, I see your point," said Brewster, nodding. "However, has it occurred to you that you might be overlooking a potential for far greater profit?"

"Indeed?" said Shannon, suddenly looking very interested.

"Well," said Brewster, "suppose I were to tell you that I know of a way for you and your brigands to at least double your profits and, eventually, perhaps to increase them even further, without having to waste all that time skulking by the trails and lurking in the hedgerows?"

"Increase our profits?" she said. "With no lurking or skulking? *How?*"

"By a process known as manufacturing," said Brewster.

" 'Man-u-facturing'?" she repeated, enunciating the unfamiliar word with care. " 'Tis some sort of sorcery?"

"Well . . . in a way," said Brewster.

Shannon sat down on the table, crossed her legs, placed her elbow on her knee, and rested her chin on her fist. "Tell me more, friend," she said.

CHAPTER
SEVEN

Warrick Morgannan was unquestionably the most powerful sorcerer in all the twenty-seven kingdoms, so powerful that he even disdained to use a magename. Wizards generally went in for that sort of thing, because there was an old belief that knowledge of one's truename rendered one potentially vulnerable to enemy adepts. While this belief was not entirely without substance, most adepts used magenames primarily because they sounded more dramatic.

In fact, all adepts had their truenames registered with SAG, as that was one of the requirements of the Guild, partly to keep track of its membership and partly to insure that there would be no disputes over magenames. If someone had already chosen Graywand or Wyrdrune and registered it, then you simply had to pick another name, no matter how much you had your heart set on it.

This sort of thing could prove rather taxing to the imagination, as the membership rolls of the Guild accounted for every adept in all the twenty-seven kingdoms and most of the good names had already been taken. If an adept died, then it was sometimes possible for his name to be passed on to someone else, but only provided that provision had been made for it in his will prior to his death and this didn't often happen. The only exceptions were generally with sons who were inheriting the business or with apprentices who had gained especially high favor. Most of the time, the magenames were simply retired and entered on the Scroll of Eternity.

Because of this system, newly sanctioned adepts often found themselves stuck for an original magename, or were so fond of the one they'd picked, only to find out that someone else already had it, that they had to settle for a number. While this practice was not encouraged, it had been adopted out of necessity. It saved the Guild Membership Committee having to come up with new magenames all the time for newly sanctioned adepts to draw out of a hat. Consequently, on the rolls of the Guild, there was now a Darkrune 4, a Blackthorn 2, and Gandalfs 1 through 6.

Warrick sounded quite properly dramatic all by itself, and with Morgannan added to it, it even sounded dashing and romantic, but that wasn't why he stuck with it. Warrick used his truename because, when he had first been sanctioned, he had wanted to ram it down everybody's throat. He had wanted to be an adept since early childhood and he had never even considered any other occupation, despite the fact that everyone had told him he had no talent. This only infuriated him and made him study that much harder.

It had taken him years to find a Guild member who would take him on as an apprentice, and then the only one who would accept him had been Batshade, a blind, arthritic, and senile old bumbler who lived in a cave and was more popularly known as Batshit, because of all the droppings covering his pointy hat and robe. It had been a miserable existence, but old Batshit had all the necessary scrolls and lab equipment, and on the days when he wasn't stumbling around the cave and raving to himself, he could actually be a pretty decent teacher. Still, Warrick had served a fifteen-year apprenticeship, when even the slowest students generally made it through in ten.

Finally, there had been some controversy over his sanctioning exam, which occasioned a debate among the Membership Committee. Some of the committee members had felt that he wasn't sufficiently dramatic with his technique, and they didn't like that he eschewed most of the traditional sepulchral chants and ancient gestures, accomplishing everything he did with a minimalist approach. In other words, they felt he lacked a certain style. However, in the end, it was decided that this was not sufficient grounds to exclude him from membership, especially since he had the secret of the Philosopher's Stone down pat, and knew all the other requisite spells as well. So they accepted him, but several members of the committee were rather condescending in their final personal evaluation remarks.

Warrick was not the type of man to overlook this sort of thing. When they asked him if he had chosen a magename, he had replied that he would use his own truename, which had raised more than a few eyebrows. "I shall be remembered," he had told them firmly, "and in time, I shall eclipse each and every one of you with my abilities. Mark well my words, for I shall be the greatest wizard of them all!"

Well, the committee took some exception to this, but they wrote off his remarks to youthful arrogance and merely gave him a lecture on proper deportment and respect for his elders. However, as time passed, they were forced to eat those words, especially in the cases of those members of the committee who had been rather harsh in their personal evaluation remarks, for Warrick had hit them each with a spell that made them go down to the Guild Records Chambers, go through all the files until they found the evaluations they had written, then stuff them in their mouths, chew them up, and swallow them. Needless to say, this display of power had not gone unnoticed and in the very next election he was voted Grand Director of the Guild. His words had proved prophetic. He had, indeed, eclipsed them all.

As Grand Director (or as the Guild members referred to him, "the G.D."), he was entitled to do things pretty much his own way. He avoided the traditional trappings of the Guild and never wore robes, but dressed in a plain, unadorned white velvet suit consisting of a high-buttoned cleric's tunic, close-fitting breeches, and matching, calf-high, velvet boots. The color went well with his long ash-blond hair, green eyes, and sharp features, but it was a most unsorcerly appearance. The most popular colors were generally murky green, deep purple, midnight blue, and, of course, blackest black, but his white suit set him apart, and in time, he became known as Warrick the White.

He had come a very long way, indeed, which only goes to show how far you can go if you apply yourself, and whatever he may have lacked in natural ability in the beginning, he had more than made up for with diligent study, perseverance, and just plain hard work. He lived for his art, and had developed powers and thaumaturgic sensitivities of a very high order, which—

"*Who's there?*" said Warrick, turning away from his massive study desk to peer anxiously over his shoulder.

"'Tis only I, Master," replied his familiar, an ugly old troll whom Warrick had named Teddy.

"I didn't mean you," said Warrick, scowling and glancing around. "I suddenly had the distinct sensation that someone was talking about me."

Teddy had been with the sorcerer ever since the day the troll had the misfortune to jump the teenaged Warrick from beneath a bridge. Trolls generally weren't very large, though they were quite strong in proportion to their size, but Teddy was a runt as far as trolls go, standing only two feet tall, with arms as long as he was high, so that his knuckles perpetually dragged upon the ground.

"Talking about you, Master?" Teddy said, glancing around. "But there is no one else here!"

Warrick frowned. "I heard a voice," he said. "But it seems to be talking about you, now."

"*Me?*" said Teddy, sounding alarmed.

He had been lurking underneath the bridge, as trolls do, when Warrick had passed by overhead and Teddy jumped him. Warrick, who was no slouch himself in the physical strength department, had pounded the living daylights out of him and then placed a spell of submission on the troll, whose hairiness and musky smell reminded him of a bear cub. Having never been given any toys or stuffed animals when he was a child, Warrick had named him Teddy and had kept him around ever since. He had tried sleeping with Teddy at first, but trolls are fitful sleepers and Teddy squirmed too much. Besides, the musky smell had a tendency to build up on you, so Teddy had been banished from the warm covers of the bed to the dust balls beneath it.

"Hmmm," said Warrick. "There are strange forces abroad in the land tonight. Voices in the ether. I don't know what the world is coming to."

He shook his head and turned his attention back to the musty scrolls spread out on his desk. From time to time, he would glance back over his shoulder again and scowl, frowning at the strange contraption that sat on the stone floor of his laboratory. It looked somewhat like a large bubble on sled runners, with a curious, shiny tube running all around it.

It was, needless to say, Brewster's missing time machine and here is how it came into Warrick's possession:

You will recall that it had been programmed to travel back into the past ten minutes for ten seconds, so that it should have appeared in Brewster's top secret London laboratory high atop the corporate headquarters of EnGulfCo International, remained in Brewster's immediate past for a scant ten seconds, and then returned automatically. However, it had not done so, because of the faulty switch in the auto-return module. Brewster had thought that he had diagnosed the flaw, but in fact, something else had happened, as well, something Brewster hadn't counted on at all.

Ripping holes in the time/space continuum can be a dicey business, and what happened was that when the machine dropped through the field of temporal disruption it had created, it experienced a sort of temporal version of an atmospheric skip, the result of an intangible temporal congruity of a universe that existed in a continuum plane parallel to our own. Now Giordano Bruno was burned at the stake for talking about stuff like this, so your narrator isn't going to push his luck by going into any greater detail. Suffice it to say that Brewster, quite by accident, had not only discovered time travel, but travel to parallel realities as well. What one might call "a real trip."

When the first time machine arrived in the Kingdom of Frank, in the Land of Darn, its temporal skip had been slightly greater than the one Brewster himself had experienced, so as a result, it had not materialized in the same place. It had actually arrived about twenty miles away from Lookout Mountain, at a somewhat greater altitude. Its parachute had automatically deployed and carried it a certain distance downwind before it landed without mishap in the middle of the road leading from Franktown, the capital city of the kingdom, through the Redwood Forest, to the town of Dudley's Port, on the coast. The first people to spot it were Long Bill, Fifer Bob, and Silent Fred, who had been serving their shift lurking in the hedgerows.

Long Bill and Silent Fred were playing chess with a little set that Fred always carried around with him, while Bob played on his little wooden fife and watched the road. He had finished off one tune and asked, "Any requests?"

"Aye, put that stupid thing away," growled Long Bill.

Bob put his fife to his lips and started playing a ribald ditty called "Put That Stupid Thing Away," which had pretty racy lyrics but lost something when it was performed as an instrumental. Besides, it wasn't what Long Bill had in mind, anyway. He fetched Fifer Bob a clout on the back of his head, which succeeded in jamming the fife halfway down Bob's esophagus.

"You sure you want to make that move?" asked Silent Fred, who spoke in complete sentences only when he played chess.

"Aye, why not?" asked Long Bill, frowning.

"Well, 'tis mate," Fred replied with a shrug.

"What? *Where?*"

"Oh, in about sixteen moves," said Fred.

"I don't like you," Long Bill groused.

"*Mmp*frrgh!" said Fifer Bob.

Without looking at him, Long Bill walloped Bob on the back and the fife was dislodged. It flew out of Bob's mouth and landed about six feet away.

"By the gods!" said Fifer Bob. "What in thunder *is* that thing?"

They turned to gaze in the direction he was looking at just in time to see the time machine bump to a gentle landing in the center of the road. The parachute collapsed and draped over it.

"*S'trewth!*" said Long Bill.

They ducked down even lower behind the shrubbery and stared at the thing fearfully for a while, but when nothing more happened, they ventured out cautiously. After a while of circling around it, they reached out to touch it hesitantly, not having any idea what to expect. Clearly, this was some sort of magical contrivance. When none of them was blasted into oblivion by contact with it, they cautiously joined efforts and dragged it off the road a short distance into the trees, where they covered it up with leafy branches.

A quick and heated debate then ensued as to what should be done about this discovery. Normally, they would have reported it to Shannon, but she was away on a scouting expedition and there was no telling when she would return. The immediate question, therefore, became how best to profit from this situation. It was quickly decided that the best way to profit from it would be to ensure a three-way split, rather than a split with all the brigands. This ran directly counter to Shannon's articles (no one knew exactly why she called them "articles," but it was generally thought she chose this term because it sounded slightly more palatable than "rules"); however, what Shannon and the other brigands didn't know could hardly hurt them. Or, more to the point, it could hardly hurt Long Bill, Fifer Bob, and Silent Fred.

A cart was obtained and then, after much perspiration and heavy breathing, they managed to lift the time machine up onto the cart, still covered with the parachute, upon which they threw a lot of mud and dirt, so that no one would think anything terribly interesting was underneath it. They then drove the cart to the residence of Blackrune 4, who was the nearest adept and lived alone in the forest about six days travel north.

All the way, they argued about how best to negotiate the deal, because concluding business arrangements with a sorcerer could be somewhat risky. Adepts, after all, could bargain from a position of considerable strength. It was finally decided to send Fifer Bob to the sorcerer's residence to initiate the dealings, while Silent Fred and Long Bill waited nearby with the cart. This decision was reached by casting lots, which meant that Fifer Bob was cast from the cart lots of times, until he finally got tired of running after it, only to be dumped off again, and agreed to undertake the task.

After some cautious negotiation, in which Fifer Bob outdid himself by describing this wonder that fell from the sky, it was arranged for Blackrune 4's apprentice to accompany Bob back to the cart and see for himself if this mysterious commodity was everything it was cracked up to be. So excited was the apprentice when he returned, for he had never seen anything like it and was convinced it was highly magical, that the deal was quickly concluded, and the three brigands went off in their unloaded cart, well satisfied with the bargain they had struck. At least, they were well satisfied until they were almost halfway home, at which point they discovered that the coins they had been paid in had turned into acorns, at which point Long Bill and Silent Fred took out their frustration on poor Bob by drubbing him soundly and shoving his fife up his nose.

Realizing they'd been had, they also realized that it would be in their best interests to keep their mouths shut about the whole thing. Not only had they botched a business deal, but they had gone against the articles and tried to cheat their comrades out of their fair share. When they returned to the Roost and, soon afterward, met Brewster, they decided it would be much wiser to keep mum about it than to tell him what they'd done. One brush with a sorcerer was enough for them. They didn't want to push their luck.

Meanwhile, Blackrune 4 used all his magic spells of divination in an attempt to find out what this strange new apparatus was. He tried one spell after another, working feverishly for days, until he inadvertently came up with one that magically tapped into the machine's temporal field and caused a sort of temporal phase loop. Unfortunately, he happened to be inside it at the time, and what happened was that the temporal phase loop pulled him through the space/time continuum field while the machine remained exactly where it was. In other words, much to the consternation of his apprentice, the machine stayed put while the wizard disappeared.

When a considerable amount of time had passed and Blackrune 4 did not return, his apprentice decided that whatever this thing was, it was far too powerful to risk having around and that it would probably be best to turn it over to the Guild. Quite aside from which, he still had several years of his apprenticeship left to serve and he'd need to see the Guild Registrar about a transfer.

So it was that Warrick, in his position as the Grand Director, wound up with the machine, for Blackrune 4's apprentice had sought an audience directly with him, certain that this strange device was so powerful and malevolent that only Warrick the White could deal with it. Besides, the apprentice figured it wouldn't hurt to get in a few brownie points with the G.D.

Warrick had questioned the apprentice extensively about everything that had happened, including which spells his master had used and, in particular, which one had effected his disappearance, and about the three strange characters who had brought the device to him in the first place. The apprentice did not know their names—for the three brigands had wisely refrained from identifying themselves—but he supposed that they had either found the device somewhere or stolen it.

To test this information, for he was nothing if not a careful adept, Warrick compelled the apprentice to step into the machine while he spoke the spell Blackrune 4 had cast just before he disappeared. And, sure enough, with a crackling of static discharges and a strange smell of ozone in the air, accompanied by a small thunderclap, the apprentice had disappeared from sight while the machine remained exactly where it was. It had not, after all, been designed to be activated by magical remote control and one can never tell what electrical appliances are liable to do if they are not operated according to instructions.

The bewildered apprentice appeared in the center of Houston Street in New York City's Greenwich Village, where his unusual appearance excited no comment whatsoever, and after an extremely confusing period of about two weeks, he wound up living with a cute nineteen-year-old performance artist and singing lead vocals in a thrash rock band. Unfortunately, his former master, Blackrune 4, had considerably greater problems in adapting to his new environment.

Busted for vagrancy in Los Angeles, he spent a great deal of time ranting and raving in the county jail, unable to understand why none of his spells would work and screaming over and over again, "I am Blackrune 4! I am Blackrune 4, I tell you!" This only complicated matters, because the LAPD assumed by these outbursts that he was confessing to being a grafitti artist and he was sentenced to thirty days in the slam and six weeks community service.

Meanwhile, Warrick continued—albeit very carefully—seeking to divine the purpose of the curious apparatus.

Clearly, it was an object of great power and whoever had made it was undoubtedly a very powerful adept, perhaps even more powerful than Warrick, for the construction of the device was baffling. This was a rather unsettling notion.

As Grand Director, Warrick knew all the senior members of the Guild and he did not think any of them would be capable of constructing such a device. It was beyond his comprehension. The curious, bubble-shaped dome looked as if it had been made from glass, but it was not glass. It was made from some mysterious substance the like of which he had never seen before. He was at a loss to explain the bright, metallic ring that encircled the device. What was it? How had it been made? What was its purpose? And if the exterior of the device was baffling, then its interior was even more so.

Warrick hesitated to enter the glasslike bubble enclosure, for he did not wish to disappear himself, but he stood outside it and looked in, his gaze traveling over the control panels and lingering on the instrumentation, and he was very much impressed. He had no idea what any of it meant, but it was easy to see that whoever had made this strange and frightening device possessed knowledge and skill that was far beyond his own. And this was not good. Not good at all.

It did not seem possible that one or more of the other members of the Guild could have secretly developed their powers to such a level. Surely, he would have known about it, for he had an extensive network of spies, assassins, and informants. He liked to keep tabs on the competition. He had also devised a spell to detect auras, so that in the event he ever encountered magic other than his own, he could read the aura of the spellcaster. He was familiar with the auras of all the senior members of the Guild, and of many of the junior members, as well, but this mysterious piece of apparatus *had* no aura. It gave off emanations of tremendous power, but he could detect no magical aura whatsoever, which meant that the adept who had constructed it had found a way to either conceal his aura or to block spells of detection. Worrisome. Very worrisome, indeed.

Warrick tried every divination spell he knew—while remaining what he hoped was a safe distance away. He tried the Postulations of Padrick the Prognosticator, the Chant of Carvin the Clairvoyant, the Divination of Devon the Determinator, and the Ritual of Ravenwing the Revenant, all to no avail. He consulted each and every ancient scroll and vellum tome he owned and nothing seemed to help. Clearly, this was some sort of entirely new kind of magic, more powerful than anything he had ever encountered or even heard of. His anxiety increased and he started losing sleep and chewing on his fingernails.

He had not told anyone else about this strange and baffling device that had come into his possession. With the exceptions of Blackrune 4 and his apprentice, who had disappeared into the unknown, only his troll familiar, Teddy, knew about it. And, of course, the three mysterious strangers who had brought the device to Blackrune 4 in the first place. Warrick wondered if anyone else knew about it. Obviously, whoever had made it knew and was probably looking for it.

There were simply too many things that Warrick Morgannan did not know. He did not know who had made the strange device. He did not know *how* it had been made. He did not know how whoever had made it was able to mask the aura of his handiwork or why no warding spell had been placed upon it, for Warrick could detect no magical safeguards protecting the device. Of course, with something this dangerous and powerful, perhaps its maker thought no protection was required. And if whoever made it was as powerful as Warrick suspected, as powerful as he (or possibly she) would have to be in order to make such a thing, then how had those three mysterious strangers managed to get their hands on it?

Somehow, he had to find those three strangers, for they were surely the keys to this mystery. He had obtained a detailed description of them from the apprentice and he had sent word to all his spies, assassins, and informants, instructing them to be on the lookout for anyone matching those descriptions. Whoever those three strangers were, they were not to be harmed. If they could not be apprehended, they were to be followed discreetly and identified, and then he would take over from there. But so far, there had been no word of them.

For hours and days on end, Warrick sat and simply stared at the device intently, as if such intense scrutiny could somehow penetrate its mysteries. At first, he thought that perhaps it might be some sort of execution device, but he had quickly discarded that idea. Why go to so much trouble merely to kill people? There were far easier ways to do that, both with magic and without, and they were numerous, so what would be the point?

Blackrune 4 and his apprentice had disappeared without a trace. No lingering auras from them could be detected, so it did not seem as if they had been transmuted somehow, or rendered invisible. But if they had not been killed or transformed, what had become of them? Where had they disappeared to?

His magic having failed him, in frustration, Warrick turned to logical deduction, a much more complicated discipline. If one stepped into the bubble-shaped dome enclosure of the device, and the device was activated, then one simply disappeared. If whoever was in the device was not killed or transmuted, then he had to be *somewhere*. So logic seemed to dictate that the strange device was an apparatus for sending people somewhere. Only where and how? And once they were sent there, what happened to them? Was there any way they could return?

Warrick could think of nothing else. He had to solve this mystery somehow and divine the secrets of this marvelous and frightening apparatus. He *had* to discover who had been responsible for its creation, for whoever it was unquestionably possessed far greater power than he did. A Guild member? Warrick did not think so. A Guild member who had attained such power could easily have deposed him as Grand Director and would not have hesitated to do so. Therefore . . . it was an adept who was *not* a member of the Guild.

And that, thought Warrick, was even more unsettling than the idea of one of the other Guild members becoming more powerful than he was, for it suggested that the creator of this device had gained his knowledge and skill independently of the Guild, without ever having served the requisite apprenticeship, or taken the exams, or being sanctioned as a practicing adept. It meant this was an unregistered adept, one completely outside the authority of the Guild. One who did not pay dues.

For someone to disregard the entire Guild so completely . . . it was simply unthinkable. It suggested that whoever this adept might be, he possessed such power that he did not consider the Guild a threat. That seemed impossible. How could anyone hope to stand against the combined powers of the Guild? Of course, the members of the Guild had never combined their powers before. There had never been any reason for them to do so, and sorcerers being a competitive lot, it had never even occurred to them to try. However, that was quite beside the point. No one adept could possibly hope to stand against all the rest of them together, no more than one man, no matter how brave and strong, could hope to stand against an entire army.

There simply had to be another explanation. Warrick racked his brain to find it. He had to solve this mystery and discover how to gain mastery over the power of the device, and the adept who had created it. He could think of almost nothing else. He had become obsessed with it.

"I am *not* obsessed," said Warrick irritably. "I am merely intrigued."

"What, Master?" said the troll.

"I said that I am not obsessed, merely intrigued," repeated Warrick.

"But, Master, I said nothing!" the troll protested, shrugging his hairy little shoulders elaborately.

"Voices," Warrick mumbled, glancing all around him. "Voices in the ether."

"But I heard nothing, Master!" Teddy said, picking his nose nervously. Trolls were gifted with a remarkable sense of smell, and when they grew anxious or nervous, they often picked their noses to clear the nasal passageways and make sure they could smell anyone trying to sneak up on them.

"Hmmm," said Warrick with a frown. "Come to think of it, I heard nothing, too. But there *was* a voice. I...*sensed* it."

Teddy's eyes grew wide, or more to the point, they grew wider, for trolls have rather wide eyes to begin with and when they get surprised, their eyes don't simply open wider, as humans eyes do, they actually move farther apart. If you're not used to it, this produces a rather disconcerting effect.

"Talking about your eyes now," Warrick said, narrowing his own in the accepted human fashion.

"My *eyes?*" said Teddy, glancing around with alarm and

picking his nose furiously. "What does it want with my eyes?"

"I'm sure I don't know," Warrick replied. "It was— . . . describing them. It seems to have stopped now."

"I'm frightened, Master."

"Nothing to be frightened about," said Warrick. "Voices in the ether cannot harm you." He frowned again. "At least, I do not think they can."

"You mean you do not *know,* Master?" Teddy asked with wonder. "But you are the most wise and powerful sorcerer in all the twenty-seven kingdoms! How can there be anything you do not know?"

"There is much I do not know, Teddy," Warrick replied. "I merely know more than most people. Yet there are some, it would appear, who know even more than I." He glanced at the time machine and scowled. "Things have been most peculiar since that time machine came into my possession. Most peculiar, indeed."

"Time machine, Master?" Teddy said.

"What?"

"You said, time machine, Master."

"I did, didn't I?" said Warrick, looking puzzled. "Time machine. . . . Time machine. . . . I wonder what it means. And I wonder how I knew to call it that."

"Perhaps the the voice told you, Master," offered the troll helpfully.

"The voice," said Warrick. "Aye . . . the voice. I sense a presence, Teddy. It seems to come and go, but most surely do I sense it."

"What sort of presence, Master?"

"An ominiscient presence."

"A god?" asked Teddy fearfully.

"A sort of god, perhaps," said Warrick, staring up at the ceiling. "Not unlike a minor deity."

"What does it do?" asked Teddy, trembling.

"I am not certain," Warrick replied, furrowing his brow. "It seems to observe. And comment. It troubles me."

He crossed the room and stood in front of the mysterious apparatus, staring at it thoughtfully.

"No, sorry, it won't work," said Warrick.

"What won't work, Master?" asked the troll.

"Calling it a mysterious apparatus. I already know it is called a time machine. Only I am not certain what that means. 'Time' I know the meaning of, but what is the meaning of 'machine'?"

He walked around it, slowly, rubbing his chin as he thought out loud.

"Machine, machine." He shook his head. "A device or contrivance of some kind? Hmmm. Time machine. A device for time?"

He was uncomfortably close to the concept of a watch, but he was on the wrong track. Besides, devices for telling time had not yet been invented.

"You mean a watch?" said Teddy.

"Don't be silly, that hasn't been invented yet," said Warrick. Then he frowned. "A watch," he said. "Now what in thunder is a watch?" He turned quickly, as if expecting to see someone sneaking up behind him. "Something very strange is happening."

"I sense nothing, Master."

"That is because you are not a powerful adept," said Warrick. "Nevertheless, it seems to be affecting you, somehow."

"It is? Make it stop, Master!"

"I am not certain if I can," said Warrick, glancing about uncertainly. "You have felt nothing, sensed nothing before this?"

"I feel nothing and sense nothing *now*, Master!"

"Hmmm. Curious. You are unaware of it, yet for a moment, you seemed affected. Perhaps because you were influenced by my own sensitivity. That could be a possible explanation. But whatever it is, it all started when this . . . this *time machine* came into my possession. Somehow, I am going to get to the bottom of this."

And chances were he would, too.

Warrick glanced up irritably. "Didn't I just *say* that?"

CHAPTER
<u>EIGHT</u>

Well, that last chapter gave your narrator a rather nasty turn. Everyone knows fictional characters are not supposed to be able to detect the presence of the narrator and start talking back to him. (This is against all the rules of good writing, just like "breaking the rule of the fourth wall," which is what happens when an actor breaks character and starts talking to the audience, or when a narrator addresses the reader directly, which is exactly what I'm doing now, so I suppose it serves me right.)

Anyway, in all the books I've written, I've never had this kind of experience before, and I don't mind telling you, I'm not quite sure what to do about it. It's pretty weird. (Not to mention potentially confusing.) However, if you look at it another way, perhaps it really isn't all that strange.

Writers are always going around talking about how their characters suddenly "take on a life of their own," or how the story starts "telling itself" and all they're really doing is writing it down as it goes along. A lot of writers tend to say those kinds of things, for some peculiar reason, as if it were a form of false modesty, like they really don't create the stories somehow, but they're only "vessels through which the wine is poured" and stuff like that. To be perfectly honest, I've always thought it was a lot of nonsense. I've written a lot of books and the only thing that's ever been poured through me was lots of beer, and believe me, *I* was the one who did the pouring. However, I'm older and wiser now and I rarely drink anything stronger than coffee, so I'm stone-cold sober as I'm sitting here pounding on the keyboard, which means I can't claim being drunk as an excuse. Frankly, this sort of thing just isn't supposed to happen.

This is going to take some thought. (Bear with me, otherwise there's no telling where this book is liable to wind up. Christ, I can hear the critics now. . . .)

As we've already discovered, the rules of reality in this particular universe are rather different from the ones we're used to, so perhaps I shouldn't be surprised. If you've got a universe where magic works, and leprechauns study alchemy, and bushes uproot themselves and start wandering about like triffids, then maybe it's not unreasonable to assume that a powerful adept can detect the presence of the narrator. I suppose it's my own fault, in a way. I wanted to make him *really* powerful, so that we could have a truly nasty villain, and I guess I simply went too far. Well, okay, that's my responsibility; I'll simply have to live with it.

So far, it seems he can detect my presence only when the story focuses on him, and even then, it seems to come and go. However, that doesn't necessarily mean his sensitivity won't increase. (Now *why* did I have to go and write that? Boy, I am just *asking* for trouble. . . .) Obviously, I'm going to have to be very careful what I write when Warrick is the viewpoint character, because he's already picked up that the "mysterious apparatus" is a time machine. He doesn't exactly know what that means yet, but he already knows a lot more than he should. (At least, he knows a lot more than he should know by this point, according to the way I've plotted the story, which means I'm going to have to really watch it or else I'll lose control completely.)

Anyway, you've been very patient through this weird digression, and by now you're probably having some serious doubts about trusting your narrator, and frankly, I don't blame you. But remember, we're all in this together, and if you haven't thrown the book across the room by now, chances are we'll make it through this thing. (I hope.) So, let's get back to Brewster, shall we?

The once-dilapidated keep had undergone a transformation. Wooden scaffolding now covered most of the tower, with people clambering all over it, tuck-pointing the stone bricks. The elevated aqueduct bringing water from upstream to the top of the water wheel had been finished and the smaller wheels powering the water lift had been installed. The buckets attached to the crude, but effective rope conveyor belt ran up the side of the tower, tipped over into the trough that filled the cistern, and traveled back down again to be refilled. While it was running, the water lift made rather pleasant, creaky, splashy sounds, and the people who had been involved in its construction watched it with fascinated admiration and no small amount of pride. Truly, it was magical and wondrous, and the spell it cast upon them was directly proportional to the amount of work they had put into it, which was considerable.

The leaching field for the septic tank had been completed. Brewster figured it would be only a matter of a week or so until he had functional indoor plumbing. In the meantime, he made sure the work crews used the latrines that had been dug an environmentally correct distance from the stream, under the supervision of Shop Foreman Bloody Bob, who was just as proud of his new title as he was of his newest and most prized possession, the bronze-mounted magic visor that not only improved his vision beyond all expectations, so that he could now identify every animal drawn on the eye chart, but gave him a most fearsome and dramatic aspect, as well.

The next project Brewster was considering was wiring the keep for electricity. He figured he could rig up a belt driven off the water wheel shaft, which was now turning with more force thanks to the aqueduct raceway dropping it a full ten feet onto the paddles. He planned to hook up the salvaged alternator from the time machine by constructing different-sized wooden pulleys, connected by a crude belt that was actually a rope plaited from vines. Mick had said this rope was very strong and held up well, which was proving to be the case so far with the water lift. To prevent the rope from slipping, Mick used a rosin made from bees' wax. Initially, Brewster figured, wire could be salvaged from the remains of the time machine, but eventually, he could show Mick how to draw it out of copper or gold, heating it and pulling it on a crank. He'd have to paint it with something for insulation, pitch, perhaps, or some other kind of substance. He didn't think any of that would present much of a problem. The problem was light bulbs. He tried explaining it to Mick.

"You see, Mick, to make a light bulb you need a small piece of wire, like I showed you, only smaller, heated to incandescence. That means it's heated to a point where it gives off a bright yellow sort of glow. The problem is, we'd need a vacuum to prevent the heated wire from burning up. I figure we could probably manage to blow some kind of glass bulb, but the trouble is getting the vacuum, you see."

"Va-kyoom," said Mick, carefully enunciating the unfamiliar word. He liked the sound of it. It sounded very magical, indeed.

"Yes, that's right," said Brewster. "Vacuum."

"And this va-kyoom prevents the wee piece of wire from burnin' up, is that it?"

"Exactly."

"Ah," said Mick. "I see."

"You do?" said Brewster with some surprise. He had expected Mick to ask for a more detailed explanation.

"Aye," Mick replied. " 'Tis a bit like a Prevent Burn spell, this va-kyoom."

"Uh . . . well, yes, I suppose so," said Brewster with a wry smile. "The only trouble is . . . well, how can I put it? I don't really have the proper apparatus here to make a vacuum."

Mick frowned. "Ah. Pity. And we must have this va-kyoom? A simple Prevent Burn spell on this heated wire would not do?"

"Well . . ." Brewster hesitated. He was, after all, supposed to be a sorcerer, and he didn't want to disillusion Mick by admitting that he didn't know any simple Prevent Burn spells. He wondered where Mick got such peculiar ideas. "I'm . . . uh . . . not really used to doing it that way," he replied.

"Sure, and I understand," said Mick, nodding. "I'm like that when it comes to makin' swords. There's some that don't finish 'em off as well as I do, and for an ordinary fightin' blade, there's really not much need for that, but 'tis a matter of craft, you see, and you like to do the job the best way you know how."

"Exactly," Brewster said, relieved and thinking that he'd have to give a bit more thought to this sorcerer nonsense. So far, it had proved helpful for these simple, superstitious people to accept science as sorcery, but it wouldn't do to have them thinking he could do absolutely anything.

"Say no more," said Mick. "I understand completely.

'Twould be beneath your dignity to resort to such a simple spell. Leave it to me.''

Brewster raised his eyebrows. "Leave it to *you?*"

"Aye. S'trewth, and I'm only a beginner, not a great sorcerer like yourself, and such simple spells are but fey magic to us little people. We do them all the time.''

"You do them all the time?'' said Brewster, raising his eyebrows.

"Aye. 'Tis no great matter.'' Mick picked up a wood splinter from the construction site and held it upright. He mumbled something quickly in a language Brewster didn't understand, and the tip of the wood splinter burst into flame. Mick mumbled something else, made a quick pass over the piece of wood, and though the flame continued to burn brightly, the wood itself was not consumed.

" 'Tis handy to light your way on a dark night in the woods,'' said Mick. "True, 'tis wood this, but I see no reason why 'twould not work with your wire.''

Brewster stared wide-eyed at the burning, yet not burning splinter. "That's a good trick,'' he said after a moment. "How'd you do it?''

But before Mick could reply, there was an alarmed cry from the keep, followed by Shannon shouting, "*Doc! Doc, come quick!*''

Thinking that perhaps someone had been injured, Brewster ran back into the keep, followed by Mick and most of the brigands on the work crew. They found Shannon in the lab, as Brewster now thought of the room where Mick kept his alchemical equipment. With all the work that had needed to be done, no one had done anything in the lab and Mick didn't like anyone going in there, so no one had disturbed the messy clutter. No one, that is, except Shannon, who had not been able to resist the temptation of the iron-banded chest left behind by the keep's former occupant.

She had picked the lock and the lid of the trunk was wide open. There was nothing inside but cobwebs, dust, and little spiders. The sole object the trunk had contained had been removed and it now sat on one of the worktables. It was a dust-covered chamberpot, made of solid gold and set with precious stones below its rim.

Shannon stood about six feet away from the table, a dagger clutched in her hand. She was staring fearfully at the chamberpot. She glanced toward Brewster and the others as they came running in, then looked back toward the chamberpot on the table.

"*It spoke!*" she said.

"What?" said Brewster.

"It cried out!" said Shannon, pointing at the chamberpot with her dagger. "*And then it spoke!*"

"Of course I cried out, you silly wench, what did you expect? You'd cry out too, if someone started poking at you with a dagger!"

"You see?" Shannon said excitedly, waving her dagger about. "It speaks! The pot speaks! 'Tis enchanted!"

Everybody looked at Brewster. Brewster, in turn, looked at everybody else. He did not, for a moment, think that the chamberpot had actually spoken. Someone was throwing their voice. He glanced beneath the table, expecting to see someone hiding under there and giggling. Maybe this was an example of brigand humor, he thought, some kind of practical joke. Maybe they were playing a trick on him to see what he would do. Maybe Shannon had something sneaky up her sleeve. Maybe they suspected that he really wasn't a sorcerer, after all.

"Is this a test?" he said uncertainly.

"'Tis Brian!" said Pikestaff Pat with awe. "'Tis the werepot prince!"

"*The werepot prince!*" the others echoed in hushed voices.

"You opened the wizard's trunk!" said Mick, looking at Shannon accusingly.

"The werepot prince?" said Shannon. "You mean Brian the Bold, the werepot prince of legend?"

"How many other werepot princes do you know?" asked the chamberpot sarcastically.

Brewster frowned. He approached the table and looked down at the pot. He bent over and peered at it intently. Then he wondered what he was looking for. Quite obviously, there couldn't possibly be any hidden little speakers. Someone in the room clearly had a talent for ventriloquism.

"If you brush some of the dust off me, you'd be able to get a better look," the pot said wryly.

Brewster jerked back. It was really startling. The voice had actually seemed to come from the pot.

"Sure, and I knew that trunk meant trouble," Mick said. "Anytime a wizard locks something away, 'tis prudent to leave it be. Faith, and I should have tossed the bloody thing in the river!"

"Oh, thank you very much," the chamberpot said sarcastically. "How would *you* like to be locked up in a trunk and tossed into a river?"

Brewster scratched his head. There had to be a point to this, a punchline or something. He decided to play along and wait for it.

"How long have you been in there?" he asked.

"Seems like forever," the chamberpot replied. "I had almost given up hope of ever getting out of there when the wench picked the lock and opened the trunk. I was about to thank her, until she started trying to pry my jewels loose with that pigsticker."

"It cried out," said Shannon as everyone turned to stare at her.

"That's because it *hurt*, you stupid trollop."

"Who are you calling a stupid trollop?" Shannon said, raising her dagger and advancing on the pot menacingly.

"Wait a minute," Brewster said, grabbing her arm, which was not the wisest thing to do, but she was so surprised he did it that she stopped and simply stared at him with disbelief. Aside from which, she did not know what a minute was and found the remark confusing.

"I can appreciate a practical joke as well as anyone," said Brewster, "but don't you think this has gone on long enough? There's still a lot of work to be done and we've all got a full day tomorrow. Frankly, I'm tired and I'm not really in the mood for pranks."

They all stared at him with puzzlement.

"Prank?" said Shannon. "What prank?"

"Well, it's very clever," Brewster said, "and whoever's doing the talking for the pot is very good, but I'm afraid I wasn't really taken in. It's a good trick, though."

" 'Tis no trick!" said Shannon. "The pot speaks! You heard! 'Tis the werepot prince!"

"Yes, yes, I heard Pat tell the story," Brewster said with a smile. "It was really quite a setup and I'm sorry if I've ruined the joke, but you didn't really think I'd fall for this, did you?"

"No, of course not," said the chamberpot. "A clever man like you? You are clearly far too wise to believe in talking chamberpots. Should have known from the start that we couldn't take in the likes of you."

"All right," said Brewster with a sigh. "Come on now, boys, enough's enough. You've had your little joke, but we still have a lot of work to do, you know."

"Yes, run along now," said the chamberpot. "Back to your chores, or whatever it is you were doing."

"Okay, now *look* . . ." said Brewster, picking up the chamberpot.

"Put me down, you oaf!"

Brewster dropped the chamberpot.

"*Ow!* Careful, you idiot!"

Brewster stared at the pot. It had felt warm to the touch, not like cold metal at all, but more like . . . like body temperature, he thought irrationally. And when it spoke, it seemed to *vibrate* slightly. . . .

When it spoke? Come on now, get a grip, he thought to himself. He shook his head, as if to clear it.

"Okay, very funny," he said with an awkward chuckle. "Now if you'll all—" His voice trailed off as he turned back toward the others. Aside from Mick, Shannon, and Bloody Bob, there was no one else in the lab. He heard the sounds of running footsteps receding through the keep.

Bloody Bob had his hand on his new sword. It was difficult to see his eyes behind the homemade prescription visor, but his mouth was drawn into a tight line. Shannon kept glancing uncertainly from Brewster to the chamberpot and back again, her body tense, poised as if she were ready to either strike or flee. Mick stood with his arms folded across his chest, his lips pursed, a thoughtful expression on his face as he gazed at the golden pot.

"It doesn't look very dangerous to me," he said. He shrugged. "Sure, and it speaks, but . . . what can it *do?*"

"You want I should cleave it in twain, Doc?" asked Bloody Bob, his fingers tightening around his sword hilt.

"*Keep that big ox away from me!*" the pot cried out.

Bloody Bob's sword rasped free from its scabbard.

"All right, now *stop!*" said Brewster.

They looked at him expectantly.

"You don't really expect me to *believe* this, do you?" Brewster asked.

"Believe what you like," said Shannon, stepping forward with a determined expression on her face, "but I'm for prying free those jewels."

"Now hold on there!" Mick said, stepping forward to block her way. "That pot happens to be *my* property!"

"*Your* property?" she said.

"That's right," said Mick. "You found it in that trunk there, which was in my laboratory, I'll have you know, and that makes it *my* property!"

"You tell her, Shorty," said the pot.

"*Shorty?*" Mick said, slowly turning back toward the pot and glaring at it malevolently.

"Step aside, Mick," Shannon said.

"You stay right where you are, Mick," said the pot. "That crazy wench is dangerous."

"I still think I should cleave it in twain," Bloody Bob said, hefting his sword.

"Right, that *does* it! Everybody *out!*" shouted Brewster angrily.

They all turned to stare at him.

"I said, 'out,' " He pointed toward the door.

Bloody Bob looked down at the floor sheepishly, then sheathed his sword and shuffled out. Shannon took a deep breath, trying to control her temper, for she wasn't used to being ordered about like this, but on the other hand, she hadn't seen this kind of firmness from Brewster before and he was a sorcerer, after all. She gave Mick a hard look, sheathed her dagger, spun on her heel, and stalked out without a word.

"You, too," said Brewster, looking at Mick.

"But, Doc—"

"*Out!*"

Mick quickly followed the others, leaving Brewster alone in the lab. With the pot.

Brewster took a deep breath and let it out slowly. "Damn,"

he said to himself. "What the hell's wrong with you, Brewster? You can't even take a joke?" He shook his head and sighed. "Hell, I wish I could get back home. This whole thing's getting on my nerves."

"Try being a chamberpot."

Brewster froze. "What?"

"I said, try being a chamberpot. I've been locked up in that bloody chest so long, I've almost forgotten what it's like not to be caked with dust and having spiders spinning webs around me. You think *you* have problems?"

"All right, this is ridiculous!" said Brewster. He started rushing around the lab, looking under benches and tables and behind shelves. "Come on out! I know you're in here!"

"I'm right here, in front of you, you dolt!"

Brewster stared at the chamberpot. There was no one else in the lab. Slowly, he approached the pot.

"Go on, come closer," said the chamberpot. "I don't bite, you know."

"This isn't happening," said Brewster. "It's stress, that what it is. I'm under too much stress. Inanimate objects do *not* talk."

"Very well, have it your way," said the chamberpot. "I'll sing instead. How's this:

"When I was lad, oh, the times that we had,
'twas nothing that we couldn't do . . .
But the best times of all, were the times when we'd call
on saucy, young Janie McDrew . . ."

"*Stop it! Stop it!*" Brewster shouted, picking up the chamberpot with both hands and shaking it.

The pot fell silent.

"What am I *doing*?" Brewster said, staring at the pot.

He put it down on the table and rubbed the bridge of his nose. "I must be losing my mind!"

"There now, 'tis not madness, never fear," the pot replied. "I had a bit of a time believing it myself, at first. And if you think 'tis hard to credit, try looking at it from *my* point of view."

Brewster swallowed hard, then reached out slowly as if to touch the pot, but drew his hand back at the last instant.

"Go on," the chamberpot said. "Touch me if you think 'twould help. I mean no harm."

Brewster reached out tentatively. It *was* warm to the touch. "Say something else," he said.

"What would you like me to say?"

Brewster pulled his hand back quickly. He moistened his lips. "I'll be damned," he said. "You really *can* talk!"

"Well now, what do you think we've been doing?" asked the pot.

Brewster shook his head with disbelief. "There has to be a rational explanation for this," he said.

"Very well," the pot said. "You tell me. Take your time. I've nowhere in particular to go."

Brewster sat down heavily on the bench behind the table. "It's impossible," he said. "How can this be happening?"

"Well, you said you heard the story," the chamberpot replied. "I understand it's gotten around a bit. 'The Legend of Prince Brian the Bold, The Werepot Prince.' I've heard it a few times, myself. Doesn't portray me in a very flattering light, I fear."

"This is simply astonishing!" said Brewster with awe. "You mean to tell me that story's actually *true?*"

"No, of course not," replied the chamberpot wryly. "Everybody knows that chamberpots can't speak. 'Tis all a lot of nonsense."

"But . . . but . . . there's no such thing as magic!" Brewster protested.

"There isn't?" said the chamberpot. "Well, you certainly could have fooled *me!*"

Brewster suddenly remembered what Mick had done outside with the wood splinter only moments earlier.

"Fey magic," he said to himself. "Mick made that piece of wood burst into flame and called it fey magic!"

"Ah, well, 'tis because he is a leprechaun," the pot said.

"A *leprechaun?*"

"Aye," the chamberpot replied. "One of the little people. You mean to tell me that you didn't *know?*"

"One of the little people," Brewster repeated slowly. "I thought he meant he was a midget! But . . . a *leprechaun?*"

"Aye, a leprechaun," the pot said, sounding puzzled. "What's a midget?"

"Well, a midget is . . . oh, now *wait* a minute! There's no such thing as leprechauns!"

"Aye, and there's no such thing as magic, and chamberpots don't speak," the pot replied. "Tell me, where do you get such peculiar notions?"

"All right, now let me get this straight," said Brewster. "Your name is Brian, and you're a prince who's been the victim of a sorcerer's spell, and Mick isn't a midget, but a leprechaun who can actually do magic, and *I can't believe I'm sitting here having a conversation with a fucking chamberpot, for crying out loud!* Oh, God. I'm either dreaming or having a nervous breakdown!"

Brewster put his head in his hands.

"There now, settle down," the pot said. "You're getting yourself all worked up."

Brewster raised his head and looked at the pot with amazement. He gave a little snort and got up, shaking his head. "I don't believe this," he said to himself.

He walked over to the window and looked out, feeling the cool night breeze on his face. There were no campfires outside and it was quiet. Everyone seemed to have left following his outburst. Probably gone back to the Roost, he thought. Makes sense. You don't want to hang around after you've annoyed a sorcerer. He's liable to turn you into something. Like a chamberpot.

"It's all a dream," he said to himself. "It *has* to be a dream."

"Aye, I said much the same sort of thing, at first," said the voice of the pot, behind him. Only, somehow, it suddenly sounded different. Brewster turned around and his mouth fell open.

There was a young man sitting on the edge of the table, with one leg casually propped up on the bench, the other dangling. He had long, curly blond hair and blue eyes, attractive features, and a slightly mocking expression around his mouth. He was dressed in tight-fitting striped breeches of brown and black, brown leather boots, a loose-fitting white blouse that laced at the neck, and a short brown velvet jacket and cape. Around his neck was a gold necklace of rubies and sapphires.

"Must be a full moon," said Prince Brian.

The battlement atop the tower had been turned into a sort of penthouse patio. Brewster had one of the tables brought up, as well as several wooden benches and stools. He had Mick and Bloody Bob bring up a couple of braziers, as they were heavy, and the result was a rather cozy, medieval, outdoor lounge that offered a very nice view.

The full moon was high in the sky and the flames in the braziers gave forth a flickering light as the gentle night wind blew. Prince Brian stood looking out from the battlement at the moonlit meadow below, while Brewster sat smoking his pipe. He had been talking with Brian for several hours and he had smoked five bowlfuls. It usually helped him relax. Usually. Tonight, it wasn't quite getting the job done.

" 'Tis good to feel the cool night breezes on my skin again," said Brian, breathing in deeply. "I had almost forgotten how it felt to be in my true form."

"How long has it been?" asked Brewster.

Brian shook his head. "A long, long time," he said. "In that dark and dusty chest, days seemed like nights. Seasons passed, countless winters turned to spring. I was unaffected by the moon's light while locked inside that cursed chest, though I suppose 'twas fortunate."

" 'Twas?" said Brewster. "I mean, it was?"

"Can you imagine what would have happened had I regained my true form while still locked within that bloody thing?"

"Oh. Yes, I see what you mean. I suppose it would be rather cramped," said Brewster.

"I do love a moonlit night," said Brian, taking a deep breath. "On nights such as these, the forces of magic are strong throughout the land. I can walk as a man again. The fairies dance and unicorns go into rut."

"Unicorns?" said Brewster.

"Aye. Pretty little beasts, but foul-smelling and mean-tempered."

"Are they dangerous?" asked Brewster.

"They can be," Brian replied, "though they tend not to bother men. However, should they see a woman, they will charge her. They don't like women. Virgins, in particular. They absolutely loathe virgins."

"Really? Why?"

"I have no idea. Perhaps 'tis something about the way they smell to them. Or perhaps because women find them winsome and want to pet and stroke them. 'Tis believed that if a virgin strokes a unicorn, she will find true love, so each spring, the woods are full of eager virgins, stalking unicorns with carrots and garlands of fresh flowers. We lose a lot of virgins that way.''

"Hmmm," said Brewster. "And you have fairies, too?"

"Oh, aye. Lots."

"What are they like?"

"Bit like nymphs, really, only much smaller and not as mischievous. About the size of your little finger, most of them. They are especially active in the spring, when the flowers bloom and they can drink the nectar. It makes them quite drunk. They flit about like maddened butterflies, smashing into one another and crashing into trees and such. But they are harmless, and they do not often venture out of the deep woods.''

Brewster shook his head. "Amazing. All this time, I had absolutely no idea there were such creatures around. I thought I'd simply traveled back into the past." He snorted. "As if time travel could be simple. But then, compared to what I've done, I suppose it is.''

" 'Tis a very strange place you come from, Doc," said Brian, turning back to face him. "Your tale strains belief."

"*My* tale strains belief?" said Brewster. "Right. This from a man who spends most of his time as a bathroom fixture.''

"Aye, but then you saw *that* with your own eyes," Brian replied. "I have only your word this place you claim to come from has castles that scrape the sky, and horseless chariots that travel faster than the swiftest stallion, and vessels that wing their way through the clouds.''

"I suppose it does sound hard to believe, at that," said Brewster morosely. He sighed. "I should probably be thrilled. I've not only succeeded in inventing time travel, but I've apparently stumbled onto the secret of interdimensional travel, as well. It's the only possible explanation. Either that, or I've died and gone to some kind of fairy-tale heaven. It's ironic. The idea of parallel universes has always been nothing more than an amusing theory, a popular theme for science fiction writers, but never something anyone took seriously. Yet, here I am. Except I'm not feeling very excited at the moment.''

"You speak words that are unknown to me," said Brian. "What is a science fiction writer?"

"A sort of storyteller," Brewster said. "One who tells tales that are very clever and fascinating, only no one takes them seriously because they're not about people in New York or Los Angeles."

" 'New York?' " Brian said. " 'Los Angeles'?"

"Cities," Brewster said absently. "Very large cities, full of people who think that living anywhere else would be uncivilized."

"Ah," said Brian. "You mean like Pittsburgh."

Brewster looked up at him sharply. " 'Pittsburgh'?"

"The largest city in Darn," said Brian. "Named for Pitt the Plunderer, though he was not its founder. He merely plundered it, then decided he liked it and chose to stay on as its ruler. 'Tis a center for commerce, knowledge, and the arts, where all roads from the twenty-seven kingdoms meet. 'Tis the most refined city in the land."

"Pittsburgh?" Brewster said, shaking his head with disbelief. "Go figure."

"Aye. 'Tis where the three rivers meet in confluence," said Brian. "A grand place, indeed. But what were those other words you said? Para-lel? Inter . . . travel something?"

"You mean parallel universes? Interdimensional travel? Hmmm. Well, that's a bit tougher to explain. I'm not sure how I could put it so that you would understand."

"Try," said Brian, looking very interested.

"Well, okay," said Brewster, taking a deep breath. "Imagine, if you can, that everything you know to be real, the earth, the sky, the stars, everything, can be contained in a single drop of water."

"Like a raindrop?" Brian said.

"Well . . . yes, but more like a single drop of water in a river," Brewster said. "We'll call this drop the universe. Now it takes a great many drops of water to make a river, but if you put enough of them together, that's what you'd have, wouldn't you?"

"Or a lake," said Brian.

"Yes, or even an ocean," said Brewster, "but let's stick with the river, because the river flows, you see, and that flow is like the passage of time. Imagine that this river is so long that it has no beginning and no end, it simply flows forever. Just as time has no beginning and no end. You with me so far?"

Brian frowned thoughtfully and nodded. "I think so. You are saying that time is like a river, with no beginning and no end, and all that we see around us—the earth, the sky, the stars—is but like a single drop of water in that river?"

"Yes, that's very good," said Brewster. "But you will remember that it takes many individual drops of water to make that river. If each drop of water is a universe—in other words, everything that we know to exist—then it follows that there are many different universes, only we don't know about them, you see, because all we know about, all we can perceive, is that which is in our own universe, our own drop of water. But all these different drops of water, these different universes, are intermingled as parts of the same river—the river of time. And though they all flow in the same river, they are still separate drops of water. They are merely so close together, and there are so many of them, that if you stand on the bank, you can never see them as separate drops. You only see the river.''

Brian was frowning with concentration as he tried to visualize Brewster's explanation.

"Think of it this way," Brewster said. "We draw a cup of water from that river. And from that cup of water, we draw an even smaller amount, merely a couple of drops."

Brewster held his right hand out flat, fingers together, palm down. "Let's say that my hand is one drop." Then he held out his left hand and placed it flat on top of his right hand. "And this is another drop. Each drop is a universe. And there are many other drops like this, layer upon layer of them, and these layers are called dimensions."

He separated his hands. "Only if we live in this dimension," he said, holding up his right hand, "there is no way for us to travel to this dimension." He held up his left hand. "Because they are like separate drops of water, you see, and while they may flow very, very close together, so close that they appear to merge, there is no *way* for them to merge, because no matter how close together they may come, they still remain separate."

He dropped his hands and shrugged, not really satisfied with his explanation, but unable to think of a simpler way to put it for the benefit of someone with no knowledge of science whatsoever.

"Anyway, that's the idea of parallel universes," he said. "How do we know that this"—he held his arms out, to encompass everything around them—"is all there is? If you had been born in that chest you were locked up in, and had lived all your life in there and never seen the outside, then you might think that the inside of that chest was your entire universe. Of course, once you got out, you'd see that there was more. Well, you're locked up in your universe, in your dimension, just like you were locked up in that chest.

There's never been any way for you to get out and see if there was anything else. You may think there is, or you may think there isn't, but because you can't get out, you can never really know for sure."

Brian put his hand up to his chin and furrowed his brow. "Only you *did* get out of your chest," he said. "And you somehow managed to enter mine."

Brewster smiled and nodded. "Yes! Yes, that's it, exactly! You understand! That's what interdimensional travel is!"

"I am not certain that I *do* understand," said Brian slowly. " 'Tis a weighty thing to ponder. But you said that this . . . this travel from one dimension to another could not be accomplished. Yet, *you* claim to have accomplished it."

"By accident," said Brewster. "I never meant to do it. I wasn't even *thinking* about doing it. I was trying to do something else entirely. I was trying to travel back into the past."

"Into the past?" said Brian. "You mean, you meant to travel from today back to yesterday?"

"Well, yes, more or less," said Brewster.

Brian frowned. "But . . ." He shook his head in confusion. "How is that possible? It cannot be done."

"That's what a very wise man named Einstein thought," Brewster replied. "Only I thought he was wrong. I believed it *could* be done. And I built a device that I thought would let me do it."

"This magic chariot of yours," said Brian.

Brewster nodded. "Exactly. Only it looks as if Einstein's had the last laugh. Maybe it can't be done, after all. At least, not in the same dimensional plane. Maybe the only way you can travel back into the past is to enter another dimension. I don't know. I don't know what happened, or how. I only know I'm here, and if I can't find that first time machine, I'll be stuck here for the rest of my life."

"Would that be so bad?" asked Brian.

"Maybe not, but I don't belong here, Brian," Brewster said miserably. "I don't even know where I am. The Kingdom of Frank, in the Land of Darn...it could be never-never land, for all I know, a fantasy land straight out of a dream. I don't even know anything about this place. I've been hanging around with a leprechaun and I hadn't even known it. Leprechauns, fairies, nymphs, unicorns... they're all creatures of myth in my world. They don't exist! And as for magic...." He exhaled heavily. "The others all think I'm a sorcerer and I let them think that because I thought it was convenient. I thought they were just primitive, superstitious people and it would be easier, and probably safer, to have them think I was a sorcerer than to try explaining the truth to them. I tried explaining it to Mick and I only wound up confusing him. Now I'm the one who's confused. And I'm certainly no sorcerer."

"But...these things you have done here," Brian said. "They are most wondrous, indeed. Are they not sorcery? And to travel from your dimension to mine, is that not sorcery?"

"It's science, Brian, not sorcery," said Brewster. "And as for what I've done here, it's just some basic engineering, not magic."

"I do not understand," said Brian, frowning. " 'Tis most puzzling. You call it science, yet it seems very like magic to me. And I know of no sorcerer who could do such things."

"That's only because they don't know how," said Brewster. "With the right knowledge, anyone could do these things. In fact, I didn't even do them, really. The brigands and the local farmers did. Mick and McMurphy and Bloody Bob and the rest. They did most of the work. I helped and I showed them how, but they were the ones who did it. I took advantage of their superstitions...well, what I *thought* were only superstitions, but there's nothing magical about any of this. They could have done it by themselves, without me. They just didn't know how until I showed them.''

Brian folded his arms across his chest and paced slowly back and forth, the wind ruffling his long blond hair. ''And you call this knowledge science?'' he said.

''Yes, that's all it is. Science is merely a form of knowledge.''

''Merely knowledge,'' Brian said. ''What, then, is sorcery?''

Now it was Brewster's turn to frown. ''I'm sure I don't know. I didn't even think there could be such a thing as sorcery.''

''Sorcery is a form of knowledge, too,'' said Brian. ''An apprentice to a wizard knows nothing when he embarks on his apprenticeship. In time, if he is diligent and clever, he learns. As an apprentice, he could not cast any spells, because he did not know how, but once he had the knowledge, he could do it. How does that differ from your science?''

Brewster grinned. ''Now you sound less like a prince and more like a philosopher,'' he said.

''What is a philosopher?''

''Never mind,'' said Brewster. ''If you thought parallel universes and interdimensional travel were confusing, you don't want to get anywhere near that one.''

''No? Well, I shall take your word for it for now. Perhaps, one day, you will explain it to me. Still, you have not answered my question. How does your science differ from sorcery, if both are knowledge?''

''Well, for one thing,'' Brewster said, ''in my world, sorcery doesn't work and science does.''

''Indeed?'' said Brian. ''Yet, your science seems to work here, in my world.''

''I see what you're getting at, but it's not the same

thing," said Brewster with a wry smile. "Just because magic seems to work here is no reason why science shouldn't. Science is merely an understanding and an application of the way natural forces work. And it isn't just one thing, really. For example, if you want to understand the life processes of living organisms, then you study the science of biology. If you want to find out more about the stars and other heavenly bodies, then it's the science of astronomy you want. Or if you're more interested in the origin of your own world, then it's the science of geology you want to study. If you want to learn about the natural laws that govern matter and energy, then it's the science of physics you're interested in, and to get more specific, there are different categories of each science, known as fields, depending on which branch of natural phenomena you wish to investigate. In physics, for example, there's mechanics, thermodynamics, acoustics, nuclear physics, particle physics, plasma physics . . ."

He saw the expression of dismay on Brian's face and stopped. "You have absolutely no idea what I'm talking about, do you?"

Brian shook his head. "At first, it seemed as if I were beginning to understand, but as you went on, it became more and more confusing."

"Well, it's pretty complicated for someone who's never had any formal education," Brewster said. "Maybe I just went too fast. It's not your fault, Brian, it's mine. I guess I just didn't explain it very well."

Brian leaned back against the wall of the battlement and scratched his head. "I wish to understand, Doc, I truly do. This science, it appears, 'tis not just one thing, but many things."

"Well, yes, in a way," said Brewster. "You see, science is basically a discipline, an approach to learning about things. But there are many different things to learn about, so the branch of science you choose depends on which specific thing you wish to learn about.''

"Ah," said Brian. "You mean like war."

"War?" said Brewster with a puzzled frown.

"Aye. If you wish to be a warrior, then you must study the art of war. But there are many different things that make up the art of war. There is the art of swordsmanship, and the art of archery, the art of disposition of the troops, and of making fortifications . . .''

"Yes, exactly! That's an excellent analogy," said Brewster.

"What is . . . analogy?"

"Oh, boy," said Brewster, rolling his eyes. "Well, it's what you just did, Brian, when you compare things that are different, but are similar in their relationships. Like war and science.''

"Ah," said Brian. "So then the many different skills that make up the art of warfare are like the different fields of science that you spoke of?"

"Yes, that's a good way of looking at it," Brewster said. "You grasp things very quickly, Brian. You're a very clever young man.''

"I *am?*" said Brian with surprise. He sat down at the table opposite Brewster, an expression of intense interest on his face. "No one has ever said that to me before. I had never thought that I was clever. Tell me more about this science! I wish to learn!''

"Well, said Brewster with a smile, "that's the most important thing you need to have to be a scientist. The desire to learn. But there's so much to learn. . . . To be a scientist means to devote your whole life to learning.''

"Then I shall be a scientist!" said Brian excitedly. "Teach me how!''

"I don't really think you know what you're asking me to do," said Brewster. "There's a great deal to learn.''

"To learn, one has to think, is that not true?" asked Brian. "Well, there is little else that I can *do* but think. I am doomed to my enchantment for all eternity, and all I have had to think of until I met you was my misery. How stupid, vain, and foolish I had been, how I had wasted my life in idle pursuits of pleasure, how I had accomplished nothing, *learned* nothing . . ."

Brian's voice trailed off and he sighed heavily as he looked up at the sky. "Soon, it will be morning, and the enchantment will take hold again. I, a prince, born of noble blood, shall once again be nothing more but the most common sort of object, meant to serve the most common and demeaning sort of purpose. 'Tis a terrible enchantment, Doc. I can feel, I can think, somehow I can speak and see and hear, but I can *do* nothing! 'Tis enough to drive one mad. And, sometimes, I think perhaps I am mad."

"Isn't there anything that can be done?" asked Brewster.

" 'Tis said that any enchantment can be broken," Brian said, "if one has the proper knowledge." He glanced at Brewster sharply. "Knowledge. Like your science!"

"Oh, now wait a minute," Brewster said. "We're talking about two different things here. Magic is not science."

"How do you know?" asked Brian.

"How do I *know?* Well . . . I . . . that is. . . ."

"You said yourself that science is but a way of knowing things about the way the world works. Well, perhaps in your world—your dimension, as you call it—magic does not work, but in *my* world, it does. Does that not make it part of how the world works?"

"Well . . . yes, I . . . I suppose you could say that," Brewster replied uncertainly.

"When an apprentice to a sorcerer embarks upon a study of the ways and secrets of magic," Brian continued excitedly, "he is said to be studying the thaumaturgic arts, which is what sorcerers call the discipline of magic. And if thaumaturgy is the art of learning how magic works, then is not thaumaturgy like a branch of science?"

Brewster stared at Brian for a long moment. "Well . . . looking at it that way . . . I suppose it would be," he said slowly.

"And you are a scientist!" said Brian. "That means you could be a sorcerer! All you lack is the proper knowledge!"

"Well . . . I don't know about that," said Brewster.

"But *I* do!" said Brian. "In my enchantment, I have passed through many hands, and among them have been the hands of sorcerers. I am no sorcerer myself, but there is much that I know about them. You teach me about your science, and I shall teach you what I know of sorcerers and their ways, and together, perhaps we may find a way for my enchantment to be broken!"

Brewster took a deep breath and let it out slowly. "Well, as a scientist confronted with a new and inexplicable phenomenon, I can hardly resist. But, Brian, there are no guarantees in science. I can't make any promises, you know."

"But you can promise to *try*," insisted Brian.

Brewster pursed his lips and thought about it for a moment. "Yes, I can promise to try."

"*Huzzah!*" cried Brian, shoving the bench back and leaping up into the air with joy. And in that moment, the moonlight faded in the early light of dawn and Brewster did a double take as a golden chamberpot came clattering down onto the stones of the battlement.

"Oh, *bollocks!*" said the pot in a disgusted tone.

CHAPTER
<u>NINE</u>

As Warrick Morgannan watched impassively, the latest "volunteer" was dragged kicking and screaming toward the mysterious apparatus.

"Time machine," mumbled Warrick under his breath.

Uh . . . right. (The sorcerer nodded with satisfaction.) Word had gotten out and it was getting more and more difficult to find volunteers. No one knew exactly what happened to the people taken into the gleaming tower of Warrick the White, located in the center of downtown Pittsburgh, but none of them was ever seen to come out again. Every time Warrick's white-caped attendants ventured out of the tower, the normally crowded streets of downtown Pittsburgh cleared in a flash.

The king had received a considerable number of protests and even several petitions demanding that he do something about this routine abduction of citizens off the streets, but there wasn't much that Bonnie King Billy could do.

King William VII of Pittsburgh was the great-great-great-great-grandson of the original Pitt the Plunderer, but he had not inherited his great-great-great-great-grandfather's brook-no-nonsense disposition. He was basically a cheerful sort, altogether a rather pleasant individual who didn't go for throwing his weight around with a lot of edicts and such, and basically pursued a laissez-faire method of monarchy. He genuinely loved his queen, Sandy, even though the marriage had been arranged by his father for political and business reasons, and he treated his subjects well, for which they had bestowed upon him the appellation of Bonnie King Billy, which he liked so much he even had it embroidered in red on the back of his black brocade dressing gown.

However, lately, the people's affection for him had waned somewhat and several new monarchial appellations were starting to make the rounds, the least offensive of which was "Bullied King Billy." He had become aware of this, primarily because the last petition he had received had been addressed to "His Not-So-Bloody-Royal-These-Days Majesty, Bonehead King Billy," and the situation was causing him considerable distress. Which was why, after thinking about it long and hard, and having a serious discussion with Queen Sandy, he had decided to pay a call on Warrick and talk to him about it.

As the panic-stricken "volunteer" screamed and clawed at the floor while Warrick's familiar, the two-foot-tall, yet extremely strong troll named Teddy, dragged him by his feet toward the mysterious—

Warrick glanced up sharply and frowned.

—the, uh, time machine, there came a loud knocking at the heavy wooden door.

"What is it?" Warrick called out, but he could not be heard over the screaming of the volunteer.

The knocking was repeated.

"Bloody hell," said Warrick. "Teddy, see if you can quiet the subject down, will you?"

"Yes, Master," Teddy said obediently. He tucked the subject's wriggling legs under one arm, then twisted around and fetched him a mighty clout on the head, which silenced his screaming. Unfortunately, it also fractured his skull and killed him instantly. "Ooops," Teddy said, looking up at Warrick with an embarrassed grin.

Warrick looked up toward the ceiling and shook his head with weary resignation. The knocking was repeated.

"Yes, yes, what *is* it?" he said, striding angrily over to the door and opening the little, sliding wooden window that was set in it at eye level. "Did I not leave word that I was not to be disturbed?" he snapped at the attendant on the other side.

"Forgive me, Master Warrick," said the worried-looking attendant, "but 'tis the king."

"What about the king?"

"He's here. And he insists on seeing you, Master Warrick. He said 'tis very important."

Warrick sighed. "Oh, very well. Tell him I'm on my way."

He slid shut the little wooden window and turned to Teddy. "Clean that up," he said with a dismissive little wave of his hand toward the corpse.

"Sorry," Teddy said sheepishly. Or, perhaps, trollishly.

Warrick opened the door and shut it once again behind him. He didn't want anyone but Teddy to know what was inside his "sanctorum," as he called his laboratory, and his servants knew better than to risk going in there. Most of them didn't even want to risk a peek. It was a well-paying job, but not without its risks. Occasionally, servants disappeared without a trace, as well.

Warrick ascended the stairs to the second floor, which was actually the first floor in the sense that the long and handsome flight of marble steps leading from the street gave entrance to it and only large iron double doors at the back, a sort of delivery entrance, gave admittance to the ground floor. He crossed the wide expanse of the ornately tiled entrance hall, with its marble columns and white-on-white decorator scheme, and went through the doors into the reception hall, where Bonnie King Billy was pacing nervously back and forth by the huge fireplace with the heavily veined marble mantelpiece.

"Your Majesty," said Warrick as he came in and gave the king a curt, perfunctory bow.

"Don't you get tired of all this white?" Bonnie King Billy said, gesturing generally at the room. " 'Tis so bright it hurts the eyes."

"I suppose I have grown used to it, Your Majesty," said Warrick.

Bonnie King Billy grunted. He was not certain quite how to proceed. He had not dressed formally for this occasion, for it was bad enough to have the king calling on the royal wizard rather than the royal wizard calling on the king, but Warrick Morgannan wasn't just any royal wizard. He was the most powerful wizard in all the twenty-seven kingdoms, with a tower that rivaled the royal palace in luxury, if not in size, and a salary that only the tax base of a city the size and richness of Pittsburgh could support. Still, powerful or not, protocol was protocol, so Bonnie King Billy had left his formal crown and royal robes at home, choosing instead to come dressed in his hunting outfit, which consisted of riding breeches, a short jerkin and cloak, and a thin gold circlet that was his traveling crown. He never actually used this outfit for hunting, for he was a very urban king and not much of an outdoorsman, but he often wore it on shopping excursions with the queen and it looked pretty snappy.

"See here, Warrick," said the king, "we, uh, need to have a talk."

"Certainly, Your Majesty," said Warrick. "What about?"

"Well, 'tis a somewhat awkward matter," said the king, hesitating slightly. "I've, uh, been receiving some complaints."

"Complaints, Your Majesty?" said Warrick, raising his eyebrows.

"Aye," said the king, "complaints. Petitions and the like. You know the sort of thing."

"Ah," said Warrick, noncommittally.

"Well . . . something must be done," the king continued.

"About what, Your Majesty?"

"Well . . . there have been, uh, certain disappearances."

"Disappearances, Your Majesty?"

"Aye, disappearances. People being snatched off the street and suchlike. You know."

"Ah. I see."

"Well . . . as I've said, there have been complaints."

"Aye, Your Majesty. You said that."

"Umm. Well . . . something must be done."

"You said that, too, Your Majesty."

"I did?"

"You did, sire."

"Umm. So I did. Well. What about it?"

"What about what, Your Majesty?"

"The disappearances, Warrick, the disappearances!" the king said irritably. "Something must be done!"

Warrick merely raised his eyebrows slightly.

"I mean . . . well . . . you must understand my position," the king said awkwardly. "I realize you have your work to do and all that, whatever it may be, but try to look at it from my point of view. I can't have your people snatching citizens off the streets in broad daylight. 'Tis damned awkward, you know."

"I see," said Warrick.

"You do?"

"I do, indeed, Your Majesty. However, I require subjects for . . . certain weighty purposes of thaumaturgical research. 'Tis most important, sire. Most important, indeed. I am afraid I cannot do without them."

"Oh," the king said. "I was afraid of that. I don't suppose you could use some sort of substitute? Cats or something?"

"Cats?" said Warrick, frowning. "I hadn't thought of using cats."

"Well, wouldn't they do?"

Warrick pondered the question for a moment. "Perhaps, but it wouldn't really be the same, sire. Besides, I rather like cats."

"Oh. Well, what about dogs?"

"There are no dogs about the streets these days, Your Majesty," said Warrick. "Your Majesty may recall his edict concerning dogs."

"Oh, that's right," the king said. "I banished dogs, didn't I? Well, the streets were becoming damn near impassable for all their droppings. The queen ruined her favorite pair of slippers, you know."

"I recall the incident, Your Majesty. But as you see, I cannot very well use dogs."

"Hmmm," said the king. "Well, 'tis most unfortunate, most unfortunate, indeed. Still, something must be done."

"What about prisoners, Your Majesty?" said Warrick.

"Prisoners?" the king said.

"Aye, sire. If I could use prisoners for my subjects, there would be no need to seek for subjects in the streets."

"Hmmm, good point," the king said. "Very good point,

indeed. That could solve the entire problem. Very well, then, you may use prisoners.''

"Then Your Majesty's sheriff will have to make some more arrests," said Warrick.

"Eh? Why's that?"

"Because I have already used up all the prisoners in the royal dungeons," Warrick replied.

"You have? Well . . . dash it all, Warrick, that makes things very inconvenient. You might have asked me, you know."

"I did not wish to trouble Your Majesty with matters of so little import."

The king grunted. "Well . . . I appreciate that, Warrick, I truly do, but if you have already used up all the prisoners, then it might take a while to fill up the dungeons once again, you know."

"Perhaps if Your Majesty sent the royal sheriff to see me, we might be able to come up with a solution," Warrick said. "A minor new edict or two might be devised, some stricter enforcement might be implemented, there's really no need for you to trouble yourself about such things. Merely give the royal sheriff your approval and it will be seen to."

"And you think that would take care of it?" the king asked.

"Undoubtedly, sire. I am sure that it would solve the problem."

"Well . . . good," the king said. "Very good, indeed. I am glad we had this little talk."

"Always happy to oblige Your Majesty," said Warrick with a smile.

The king left, satisfied. However, he would not remain that way for long. His easygoing, laissez-faire method of monarchy was about to undergo considerable modification, which would make the royal sheriff very happy, for it would give him a great many new edicts to enforce, very strict edicts that Warrick would diplomatically suggest and that the royal sheriff would eagerly implement in the king's name. Being even slightly late with revenues, spitting on the street, public drunkenness and lewd behavior, not having proper change for the tollgates, and a host of other things that most citizens of Pittsburgh had never thought twice about would suddenly become crimes punishable by immediate imprisonment and the dungeons would provide Warrick with a steady supply of subjects for his thaumaturgical research. And poor, bumbling King Billy would bear the brunt of the people's resentment.

"There is, of course, another way," said Warrick, looking up toward the ceiling. "A certain voice in the ether could supply me with the answer to the riddle of the so-called time machine."

Unfortunately, the narrator couldn't really do that, because it would cause serious interference with the plot.

"Well, in that case, 'poor, bumbling King Billy's' predicament would be the narrator's responsibility and not mine," said Warrick.

Nevertheless, it was Warrick who came up with the idea of instituting strict new edicts to fill the royal dungeons with prisoners he could use as his subjects.

"Perhaps," said Warrick with a sly smile, "but 'tis your plot, unless I am mistaken."

Back at the keep (and not a moment too soon), Brewster hadn't slept a wink all night. He'd been on adrenaline overdrive, talking to Brian and trying to assimilate everything he'd learned. Suddenly, it was a brand-new ball game. In a brand-new ball park, so to speak. The trouble was, the rules were slightly different here. In this stadium, the runners didn't steal third base, they waved their fingers at it and made it disappear. The bat boys were leprechauns, the team mascot was a unicorn, and the fireflies hovering over center field were actually fairies. (And having belabored that analogy to death, we should probably move on.)

After Brian's enchantment had kicked in again, Brewster had carried him downstairs to the kitchen of the keep—which, he'd decided, would be the next area in need of modernizing— and they talked until the sun came up. Brewster heated some water and made himself some tea from an herbal mixture Mick had given him. It tasted rather lemony and was about ten times more stimulating than coffee. It had the effect of keeping Brewster wide awake—*very* wide awake— and giving him a nervous energy that would have kept him up for the next forty-eight hours even if he wasn't too wound up to sleep.

Brian had been a great deal easier to deal with as a handsome prince than as an ornate chamberpot, and not only because it felt a lot more natural to talk to a person than to an appliance. (Or was it a utensil? Anyway, you get the general idea.) As a chamberpot, Brian was somewhat caustic and sarcastic, not that Brewster could really blame him, and though his personality didn't really change in any significant way, there was an edge to him that took some getting used to.

In fact, the whole idea of man turning into an object took some getting used to. Talking with him while he was in his enchanted form was positively surreal and a graphic reminder of the sort of world Brewster had wound up in. Though several weeks had passed, Brewster hadn't really seen anything that would have led him to suspect he had been transported to another universe in some kind of parallel dimension. The peregrine bush, he realized belatedly, should have been his first clue, but he had merely assumed it was some rare plant, perhaps some sort of localized mutation, that had not survived into the modern age he came from.

He had seen nothing of the creatures Brian had mentioned, unicorns and fairies and nymphs, and while the existence of such creatures might have seemed improbable, he had little difficulty believing they existed after seeing a chamberpot turn into a man and back again.

Brian had told him all about how he had wound up being enchanted. His version of the events leading up to his current predicament closely followed the legend related by Pikestaff Pat, and Brian told it with a surprising amount of candor.

Following his disappearance from the palace, after he'd been stolen by one of the palace servants, Brian had passed from hand to hand, often fairly rapidly, as those into whose possession he fell became aware that he was no ordinary chamberpot—and not just because he was encrusted with gems. The people of the twenty-seven kingdoms were extremely wary of enchanted artifacts, and rightly so. Adepts were always experimenting with strange new spells and it was not uncommon for such spells to be dangerous, or even to go wrong somehow.

At first, Brian had raged at his successive owners, and then pleaded with them, begging to be taken to a sorcerer who could reverse the spell, but it was all to no avail. As soon as people found out their new, ornate chamberpot could talk, they couldn't wait to get rid of it, jewels or no jewels. And as the legend of the werepot prince grew, passed on by his former owners, adepts became aware of it and grew highly interested in finding him. A number of them did.

At first, Brian had seen this as a sign of hope, because he knew his father would reward any adept who could restore him. However, no adept had ever succeeded in breaking the enchantment. Worse still, none of them would return him to his family, for to do so would have meant admitting they had failed to restore him to his rightful form. None of them had wanted to admit that another adept had devised a spell he couldn't break. Brian had found this particularly frustrating, because the result was that he spent a great deal of time languishing in storerooms, trunks, and secondhand shops.

He eventually had become more or less adjusted to his fate, if not totally resigned to it. Though he may have been spoiled and pampered by his family, Brian was an intelligent young man, as Brewster had already observed, and his anger and bitterness over what had happened to him frequently manifested itself in a personality that could be highly ascerbic and sarcastic. In other words, as Pikestaff Pat had put it, Brian could be a royal pain to those who came in contact with him.

Adepts did not take kindly to such behavior. Having failed to restore him to his proper form, they generally concluded that there was no profit in a talking chamberpot, regardless of its value as a curiosity, and little point in keeping it around. Especially if it was going to be abusive. So they either unloaded him on someone else, or if Brian had really gotten on their nerves, they tried destroying him.

"*You mean they actually tried to kill you?*" Brewster said.

"Life is cheap to most adepts," Brian replied, "so long as 'tis someone else's life. Aye, they tried to kill me, some out of spite, some out of fear that I would tell others their powers had not been sufficient to restore me. But 'twas not so easily accomplished. I was beaten with large hammers, thrown from great heights, tossed down wells, struck with axes, once I was even thrown into a fire in an attempt to melt me down."

"My God!" said Brewster. "How horrible! How on earth did you survive?"

"Ah, 'tis the nature of the enchantment, you see, that I cannot be destroyed," Brian replied. " 'Twas meant I should suffer throughout all eternity. Pound me with hammers from now until the end of time and you shall not make a single dent. Toss me down a well and I shall float until some peasant comes along to fish me out. Strike me with the sharpest axe, yet you shall fail to split me. Toss me into a blacksmith's forge, yet no matter how fierce the heat, I simply shall not melt. I may blacken somewhat, but wipe me off and I shall look as good as new. Oh, but I shall feel the pain of it! Though I may not be allowed to perish, I am indeed allowed to suffer pain."

"That's the most awful thing I've ever heard!" said Brewster with chagrin. "God, you poor kid!"

"Well, I thank you for your sympathy," said Brian, "but sadly, sympathy shall not break this damnable enchantment."

"No, I don't suppose it will," said Brewster. He took a deep breath and exhaled heavily. "Frankly, Brian, I just don't know what I can do. I've never encountered anything like this before. I know I promised that I'd try to help you, but . . . in all honesty, I don't know how I can."

"Well, 'tis grateful I am that you promised to make the attempt," said Brian.

"Attempt? I wouldn't even know where to start," said Brewster. "If *real* sorcerers couldn't break the spell, I don't see how *I* could. I'm not a sorcerer, I'm merely a scientist."

"Nay, not *merely* a scientist, Doc," said Brian. "You must be a very great scientist. Has any other scientist ever succeeded in doing what you have done, whether by accident or by design? Has any sorcerer? Where sorcerers have failed, perhaps a scientist may succeed."

"I wish I had your confidence, kid," said Brewster sadly.

"You have done things no sorcerer could do," Brian assured him. "You can use your . . . what did you call it, your method?"

"Scientific method," Brewster said.

"Aye, you can use your scientific method to study thaumaturgy, and thereby divine the secrets of the thaumaturgic arts."

"I don't know," said Brewster dubiously. "Wouldn't it be better if we just got a bunch of sorcerers to put their heads together and see if they couldn't find a way to—"

"Nay, Doc, nay! 'Twould be disaster! You must keep away from sorcerers, else . . ."

Brian's voice trailed off. "Else what?" asked Brewster.

The chamberpot remained silent.

"Brian?"

A soft sigh came from the pot. "We need each other, Doc. I need you because you may be my last hope to break this enchantment and live a normal life. And you need me because there is much about this world you do not know, and would not understand."

Brewster stared at the chamberpot and frowned. "I'm not sure I understand now. Why should I keep away from sorcerers? Is there something you haven't told me, Brian?"

For a moment there was no reply, and then the pot sighed once again, a strange, tinny sort of sound. "Aye, Doc, there is. Faith, and I do not wish to tell you, for I do not mean to frighten you, and yet, 'twould be best if you were to know the truth."

"What truth?" asked Brewster uneasily.

"The people here believe you are a mighty sorcerer," said Brian, "and I fear 'twould not go well for you if you were to admit the truth."

"Well, I could explain it to them and surely they would—"

"Nay, Doc, you do not understand. You must *never* tell

them the truth. You must never tell *anyone*. Your very life depends upon it."

"My *life?*" said Brewster. "Surely, you don't think they'd *kill* me?"

"Perhaps not," said Brian. "But 'tis not the brigands nor the local farmers from whom you have the most to fear. 'Tis the Guild."

"The Guild?" Brewster frowned.

"Aye, SAG, the Sorcerers and Adepts Guild," Brian said. "You see, when these people here first met you, they took you for a mighty sorcerer, and in your innocence, you allowed them to believe that. You did not know that there was such a thing as sorcery, nor did you know about the Guild. Had you but known, you never would have allowed them to mistake you for a sorcerer, no matter how hard 'twould have been to convince them of the truth."

"Somehow, I suddenly have the feeling I'm not going to like this," Brewster said.

"I fear 'tis so," said Brian. "You see, Doc, the Guild is a body of adepts united in a common cause, to govern the practice of sorcery. Its Council of Directors is made up of the most powerful adepts in all the twenty-seven kingdoms, and the Grand Director of the Guild is Warrick Morgannan, called Warrick the White, the most evil, dangerous, and powerful adept of them all. And 'tis law that all adepts must be members of the Guild, and submit to its authority."

"You mean it's like a union?" Brewster asked.

"Aye, 'tis a union of adepts," said Brian, "all adepts in all the twenty-seven kingdoms. No one may practice sorcery without being a member of the Guild."

"So what are you telling me?" asked Brewster. "I'm a scab?"

" 'Scab'?" said Brian, puzzled.

"Never mind," said Brewster. "Go on."

" 'Tis a lengthy and most difficult process, becoming an adept," said Brian. "You must first find an adept willing to take you on as an apprentice, and that adept must be a member of the Guild. As an apprentice, you must serve your master faithfully, and spend your every waking hour in the study of the thaumaturgic arts. Many of its secrets you must discover on your own, and when your master feels that you are ready, the Guild will test you.

"Should you pass the test," Brian continued, "you will be elected to the Guild and you may then call yourself an adept and practice magic. Should you fail to pass the test, you must either forsake your goal of becoming an adept or remain an apprentice to your master until such time he feels that you can take the test again, though if you fail, 'tis a bad reflection on your master and odds are you will be punished. You may never be allowed to take the test again, and you may be forced to spend the remainder of your life as an apprentice. Or possibly as something much less pleasant, say a toad or . . . well, perhaps even a chamberpot. 'Tis very strict, the Guild is. They are especially strict concerning those whom they allow to call themselves adepts and practice magic. The penalties for pretending to be an adept, or calling yourself a sorcerer if you are not a member of the Guild, are quite severe."

Brewster moistened his lips nervously. "*How* severe?"

"Believe me, you do not wish to know," said Brian. "I am but a small example of how imaginative an adept can be when he decides to punish someone. And it could have been much worse, you know. *Far* worse."

Brewster swallowed hard. "I see. Well, all the more reason to clear things up, then. I have enough problems without getting a sorcerers guild mad at me. The sooner I tell everyone the truth, the better."

"Nay, Doc, 'tis much too late, I fear," said Brian. "By

now, everyone in Brigand's Roost and all the surrounding farms believes you to be a powerful adept. I doubt they would understand the truth. More likely, 'twould frighten and confuse them.''

''It didn't frighten or confuse you,'' said Brewster.

''*I* frighten and confuse them,'' Brian said. ''You saw how they ran. Yet even were they not to become frightened, they would have a hard time believing you. You tried telling the truth to the leprechaun and what was the result? Nor did you tell him the entire truth, for you did not know it at the time. You told him you came from a future age and this only convinced him further of your powers as a sorcerer. What would he think if you told him you came from another world, from another dimension?''

''But I was able to explain it all to you,'' said Brewster, ''even if it did take all night, you finally understood.''

''Aye, 'tis true, perhaps the leprechaun might understand as well, but can you vouch for all the others? Though what you have done here may be science, 'tis sorcery to all the others and the Guild would look on it as sorcery, as well. Even if you could convince them that science and sorcery are different things, they would see your science as a threat to their own power. And anything that would threaten the power of the Guild is eliminated by the Guild. Quickly, and most decisively.''

''Great,'' said Brewster with a sour grimace. ''So what am I supposed to do?''

''You must keep up the pretense, for your own safety,'' Brian said. ''You must avoid adepts. Tell the others, the brigands and the farmers hereabouts, to say nothing of your presence here to anyone.''

''What . . . what reason should I give?'' asked Brewster.

''Tell them you require solitude,'' said Brian, ''to pursue the perfection of your art. Tell them you have grown weary of towns and cities, with their crowds and ceaseless noise, and that 'twas your decision to remain here for the peace and quiet of the Redwood Forest. They will understand this, and so respect your wishes. Adepts command respect because adepts are feared. 'Twould not be safe for you to take away their fear.''

"But . . . what about my missing time machine?" asked Brewster. "Unless I find it, I'll never get home. I can't just stay here and hope that it turns up somehow. If someone doesn't bring me word of it, I'm going to have to start looking for it myself."

"Are you certain your time machine is here?" asked Brian.

"It *has* to be here somewhere," Brewster replied. "If it's not . . . then I'll never get home."

"Then we must try to find it somehow," Brian said. "I shall try to think of something."

"Yes, but I'm afraid that's not going to help you," said Brewster with a sigh.

"Perhaps it may," Brian replied, "if you were to take me with you to your world."

"Take you *with* me?"

"Aye," said Brian. "You said there is no magic in your world. If that be true, then perhaps the enchantment will not hold there."

Brewster nodded. "Maybe. I suppose that's possible. Only what if it doesn't work that way?"

"What have I to lose?" asked Brian.

"You have a point," said Brewster. "Okay, kid. It's a deal."

There was a loud knocking at the door. Brewster picked the pot up and tucked it under his arm, then went to open the door. The little peregrine bush came shuffling in, dragging Mick along on its rope leash. It started rubbing its thorny little branches against Brewster's legs.

"*Ouch!*" said Brewster, backing away. "Stop that!"

The little bush rustled backward a few feet, its branches drooping slightly.

"It seems to have taken a likin' to you," Mick said. "Dragged me all the way over here, it did." He grimaced sourly. "I see you still have the werepot."

"Mick, this is Prince Brian," Brewster said. "Brian, this is my friend Mick." He blinked and shook his head. "Look at this, I'm introducing a leprechaun to a chamberpot."

"Greetings, Mick," said Brian. "I'm sorry I called you Shorty yesterday."

Mick merely grunted and gave a curt nod.

"You could accept his apology, you know," said Brewster, trying to play the peacemaker. "He is a prince, after all, and princes don't usually apologize, do they?"

Mick grunted again. "I accept your apology," he said gruffly.

"Thank you," Brian said.

Mick grunted a third time. " 'Tis most civil it's bein' this mornin'."

"*He's* being," Brewster corrected him. "He is a person, you know. In fact, he really *was* a person last night. It was a full moon."

"So that part of the legend's true, then?" Mick said with interest.

"Aye, most of the legend's true," said Brian, "save for a few embellishments that some have added to the story."

"I promised Brian I would try to help him," Brewster explained.

"Can you?" Mick asked.

"I honestly don't know," Brewster replied, "but I promised him I'd try." He glanced outside. "You're alone?"

"Aye, none of the others came," said Mick. "Scared off, they were."

"You see?" said Brian. "I told you that I frightened them."

"Oh, 'tis not for fear of you they didn't come," said Mick. " 'Twas for fear of the dragon."

" 'Dragon'?" Brewster said.

"Aye, the dragon."

"*What* dragon?"

"The one sittin' up there on the tower," Mick replied, pointing up.

CHAPTER
<u>T E N</u>

For a moment that seemed to hang in eternity, Brewster
stared at Mick, standing there just a couple of feet or so
inside the open doorway with his peregrine bush on a leash,
and thought that he was joking. Then *hoped* that he was
joking. Hoped very, very hard. Only the expression on
Mick's face was not the deadpan look of someone pulling
someone else's leg. It was the normal expression of someone mentioning something he'd just seen and did not find
especially remarkable, the look of someone who'd just
glanced up at the clouds and said, "I think it's going to
rain."

"A *dragon?*"

As if he were sleepwalking, Brewster moved past Mick
and stepped up to the open door. He wasn't sure what he'd
intended. Perhaps he had intended to step outside, walk out
into the yard, and look up at the tower, but he never got any
farther than the threshold, for what he saw through the open
doorway was the shadow of the keep's tower angling across
the yard, and right about where the shadow of the tower

should have ended, there was *another* shadow, a shadow of something very large, with huge, reptilian wings.

Brewster reached out with his right hand, took hold of the door, and gently closed it. Then he turned around and leaned back against the door. His knees felt weak and his mouth had gone completely dry.

Something clanged loudly on the floor and a voice cried out, "*Ouch!* Doc!"

Brewster had dropped the chamberpot. He bent down and picked it up.

"I'm sorry, Brian," he said in a dull voice. He clutched the chamberpot to his chest with both hands and looked at Mick.

"Is that..." he started, but his voice had broken and sounded extremely high. He shook his head, cleared his throat, and tried again. "Is that... really... a *dragon?*"

"Aye," said Mick simply.

"How..." His voice broke again and came out soprano. He cleared his throat with a deliberate effort. "How... *long*... has it been... up there?"

"Sure, and I don't know," said Mick. "It was sittin' up there when I came." He frowned. "You didn't know about it, then?"

"No," said Brewster, his voice coming out in a high squeak again. He cleared his throat hard, three times in succession. "Didn't that..." He fumbled for words, and then settled for simply pointing up toward the ceiling. "... strike you as... rather *unusual?*"

Mick merely shrugged. "Sure, and I thought you must have summoned it."

Brewster cleared his throat again. "It... you... weren't ... frightened?"

"What, of the dragon?" Mick said. He shrugged again. "Why should I be? Dragons don't eat leprechauns."

"Oh," said Brewster. "What about . . . people?"

"Sometimes," Mick said. "They prefer cows, though. More meat on the bones."

"Ah," said Brewster, nodding. "I see."

"You didn't summon it, then?" asked Mick, speaking as if seeing a dragon sitting up on your neighbor's roof were a perfectly normal occurrence.

"Noooo," said Brewster, swallowing hard. He handed the chamberpot to Mick. "Hold on to Brian for a moment, will you?"

Mick took the pot and Brewster ran upstairs to his bedroom, just below the battlement of the tower. As he ran into the room, he could see a large, scaled tail flicking back and forth, just outside the window.

"Oh, boy . . ." he said. "Oh, boy . . . keep calm, now, just keep calm. . . ."

He tiptoed over to the bed, reached down underneath it, and slid out the pack that contained his emergency supply kit, which he had pulled out of the time machine just before the fuel tanks had exploded. Glancing up at the window, as if expecting some giant clawed hand to come reaching in for him, he fumbled inside the pack until his fingers felt what he was looking for. He pulled out a snub-nosed stainless-steel revolver and a box of cartridges.

His hands trembling, he opened the cylinder and started loading it. He loaded all six chambers, then closed the cylinder. It was a .357-caliber Smith & Wesson Combat Magnum, specially polished and engraved, with a two-and-one-half-inch barrel and pearl grips, one of a matched pair he had been presented with by the CEO of EnGulfCo International, who was also on the board of Smith & Wesson. Its companion revolver was an equally fancy .38-caliber Chiefs Special, which he had packed in the emergency supply kit of the original time machine. He hadn't really thought that he would ever actually have need of it, but it seemed like the sort of thing an emergency supply kit should contain, so he'd opted for the smaller caliber, less intimidating gun at first. However, the .38 was now in the missing time machine, and as he gazed down at the loaded, snub-nosed .357 in his hand, he was suddenly very glad he had the more powerful one. Nevertheless, it seemed very small compared to what was sitting on the tower just above him. Brewster was suddenly painfully aware of his lack of experience with firearms.

He had only gone shooting once before, when the CEO of EnGulfCo took him to the range to "try 'em out." He had instructed Brewster in the use of the matched revolvers, giving him a short lecture on gun safety, proper sight alignment, trigger control, and so forth, and Brewster had turned in a game, if not quite adequate performance. Actually, he had gotten quite a kick out of shooting them, but the guns had made Pamela nervous and he'd put them away.

"Are you goin' up to see it, then?"

Brewster jumped about a foot and almost dropped the gun. He took a deep breath and turned around. "Dammit, Mick," he whispered harshly, "don't *do* that!"

"Why are you whisperin'?" asked Mick, coming into the room with the chamberpot tucked under his arm.

Brewster merely pointed toward the ceiling.

"Ah," said Mick. "You're plannin' to sneak up on it and blast it, like you did Robie McMurphy's foolish bull?"

Brewster looked down at the revolver in his hand. What the hell *was* he planning to do? Suppose bullets didn't work on it? Suppose it was magical and invulnerable to gunfire? Suppose it breathed fire?

He glanced up at Mick and his gaze focused on the chamberpot. "You didn't tell me about *dragons!*" he accused Brian.

"Didn't think of it," said Brian. "You don't see many of them about these days. They're quite rare, really."

"Not rare enough, if you ask me," said Brewster. "What the hell are we supposed to *do?*"

"You might ask it what it wants," suggested Mick.

"*Ask it what it wants?*" said Brewster.

"Aye," said Mick.

"And I suppose it'll answer me," said Brewster. "No, never mind, don't say anything. It talks, right?"

"Aye, it speaks," said Mick. "You've never met a dragon before, then?"

"Actually, no, I haven't," Brewster said. "This'll be my first." He snorted. "What am I *saying?* I'm not going up there!"

"Good morning," said a loud, deep voice just outside the window. It sounded a cross between a human voice and a threshing machine.

Brewster jumped and spun around, raising the revolver. He found it difficult—no, he found it *impossible* to keep his hands from trembling.

"Well, now that's not very friendly, is it?" There was a large head just outside the window. Brewster couldn't see all of it. Just a huge yellow eye and some iridescent scales. "Do you always threaten your visitors with a gun?"

Brewster stared at the fearsome yellow eye and tried to will himself not to be afraid. And then, suddenly, something occurred to him. He lowered the revolver slightly and frowned. He glanced from the revolver to the dragon's eye outside the window. "You know what this *is?*" he said with surprise.

"Of course, I know what it is," the dragon replied. "It's a revolver. And a rather small one, at that."

Brewster lowered the gun. He lowered his jaw, as well.

"Oh, come on up," the dragon said impatiently. "I am

not going to hurt you, but I *am* getting a crick in my neck, looking down like this.''

The head disappeared.

Brewster shook his head. "I don't believe this." He dropped the gun on the bed, took off his glasses, and rubbed the bridge of his nose. "No, this is too much! I don't care what happens, *this* I've got to *see!*"

He ran up the stairs to the top of the tower, with Mick following close behind.

The dragon was sitting perched on the wall, its talons dug into the stone. Brewster stood and simply stared at it with openmouthed astonishment.

It was about the size of an eighteen-wheeler, with a long tail; huge, batlike, leathery wings; gleaming, iridescent scales; and a large, triangular-shaped head on a long neck. It was lapping water out of the cistern, like a dog drinking from a toilet bowl, only much louder.

"Jesus Christ," said Brewster.

"No, Rory," said the dragon.

"'Rory'?" Brewster said.

"Actually, it's only a nickname," said the dragon. "Human throats cannot make all the sounds necessary to pronounce my given name. Rory is sort of an abbreviation. How do you do?"

"Uh . . . fine, thank you," Brewster said weakly.

"And you are?"

"Uh . . . Brewster. Dr. Marvin Brewster. But my friends just . . ." His voice trailed off. "My God, you really are a *dragon!*"

"Allow me to compliment you on your powers of observation, Doctor," Rory said wryly. "I see you have company. I hope I haven't dropped in at an inconvenient time."

"Oh . . . uh . . . no, that's . . . quite all right," said Brewster.

"Uh . . . this is my friend Mick O'Fallon, and . . . uh . . . the chamberpot he's holding is actually Prince Brian the Bold."

The dragon nodded. "Always happy to greet one of the little people," it said. Then it squinted at the chamberpot. "Prince Brian, eh? I see you've run afoul of Caithrix."

"That's the wizard who enchanted me!" said Brian. "How did you know?"

"I can smell his aura on you," the dragon said. "Caithrix always had an especially pungent aura."

"Had?" said Brian.

"Well, he's been dead these past one hundred years or so."

"One hundred *years?*" said Brewster, staring at the chamberpot.

"Is that a long time?" asked Brian.

"You don't look a day over eighteen!" said Brewster.

"One of those 'for all eternity' enchantments, eh?" the dragon said. "You must really have annoyed him. Although Caithrix always did annoy rather easily. Arrogant little adept, he was. Even disdained to use a magename, just like his grandson, Warrick."

"Warrick the White is Caithrix's *grandson?*" Brian said.

"His daughter Katherine's son," the dragon said. "Even more arrogant than his father was, doubtless because he was born a bastard and felt he had a lot to prove."

"Katherine's son?" said Brian. "Born a . . . then that means . . . Oh, gods! Warrick the White is my *son?*"

"Ah," the dragon said. "That would seem to explain your current predicament."

"I can't believe any of this," said Brewster. "And I had to leave my video camera behind!"

"Pity," said the dragon. "I would have enjoyed seeing a videotape of myself. Though I am not entirely certain it would work, you know. I am not sure if you can photograph magical creatures."

"Wait a minute," Brewster said. "You *know* about video? And you knew a revolver when you saw it! *How?*"

"Oh, I know all about your world," Rory replied. "I have seen it often in my dreams. Dragons dream in different dimensions, you know."

"In black and white or color?" Brewster asked, repressing a sudden urge to giggle.

"In color, of course," Rory replied. "I hope you don't mind my dropping in like this and taking a drink from your cistern, but I was merely passing by on my way back home and I could not help noticing what you've done here. A water lift, an aqueduct, a nice job of tuck-pointing on the stonework . . . I really like what you've done with the place."

"Uh . . . thanks."

"I merely wanted to pop in and say hello. I have never met anyone from the dream dimensions before. However did you manage to cross over?"

"Well . . . that's rather a long story," Brewster said.

"Excellent!" the dragon said with a rumble of contentment. "I do so love a good story!"

MacGregor the Bladesman, better known as Mac the Knife, stood outside the cottage of Blackrune 4, looking very grim. It was actually a rather sizable dwelling for a cottage, since its former occupant had been a wizard, after all, but it was still basically a cottage, complete with thatch roof and wooden shutters, garden, whitewashed picket fence, and all the cozy accoutrements. Sort of an upscale cottage.

Mac and his men had ridden quite a long way, all the way from Pittsburgh, and they were tired and dusty from their journey. Fortunately, while en route, they had been set upon at least three times by various groups of highwaymen and ruffians—four, if you counted the ones who recognized their mistake before they got too close and ran like hell—and these slight diversions had served to break up the monotony of what would otherwise have been a rather dull and tiresome trip.

"Anything?" said Mac as his three henchmen came out of the cottage.

The men simply shrugged. They bore a strong resemblance to one another, which was only proper, as the three of them were brothers.

Mac gave a low grunt and frowned. "Well, I suppose 'twas too much to hope for," he said.

He had a wonderful speaking voice, deep, melifluous, and very manly, and if he had been born about a thousand years later, and in another dimension, he could have had a great career as a radio broadcaster or a Shakespearean actor, or perhaps dubbing the voices of malevolent villains in science fiction films.

He could also sing and play guitar, and those talents, combined with his rugged, virile good looks, set many a female heart aflutter. He had dark, curly hair; a handsome beard that he kept nicely groomed and trimmed, unlike the facial forests sported by most of his contemporaries; and he had dark, piercing brown eyes that could either flash with merriment or glower with malevolence. His features were ruggedly angular, with a square jaw, a straight and well-shaped nose, and good cheekbones. . . . In short, he was a darn good-looking guy. (Or a good-looking guy from Darn, take your pick.) He was a manly man with a massive, six-foot two-inch frame and a likable, charming disposition. The fact that he also happened to be a professional assassin was purely incidental.

Sean MacGregor looked upon it as a job and nothing more. Whenever he was asked why he chose this particular occupation, he would simply shrug and say, " 'Tis a gift." And 'twas, too. He was remarkably good at it.

He was an accomplished swordsman and had yet to meet his match, but as good a swordsman as he was, he was even better with a knife. His prowess with knives of all shapes and sizes was legendary. It was said that he could trim the wings of a fairy in flight, which was actually an exaggeration, because fairies could outfly just about anything, from hummingbirds to bees, and Mac had never even attempted the feat. He could, however, draw one of the many knives he wore in his crossed leather bandoliers and hurl it with such lightning speed that the eye could hardly follow it. He unfailingly hit wherever he aimed it, nor was he particular about whether he hit it from the front or from behind. Assassination was assassination, and Mac didn't allow any sporting sensibilities to interfere with his job. He was, after all, a professional.

Unlike many cheap, lower grade, nonguild assassins, who were often very good at skulking and being generally sneaky, but whose fighting prowess varied widely, Macgregor proudly wore the guild badge of his profession on his brown, rough-cut leather tunic. The badge was a tasteful silver dagger pin, four inches long, two inches wide at the crossguard, with an inch wide blade tapering to a sharp point. He wore it pinned to his breast, over his heart, and it identified him as a member in good standing of the Footpads and Assassins Guild, and anyone who valued their life knew better than to abbreviate that into an acronym.

For a long time, there had been a movement in the Guild to shorten the name simply to Assassins Guild, but many of the old guard professional assassins did not wish to have their occupation demeaned by having a guild called the Assassins Guild that also admitted footpads, however necessary they might be to the profession as auxiliaries. An alternate proposal had been made to reverse the order of the names, and have it be known as the Assassins and Footpads Guild, but the footpads liked having top billing, and since there were many more footpads than assassins, they kept voting it down at the annual meetings. It was a problem. Assassins who were members of the guild usually circumvented it by referring to themselves as pros, and everyone else, regardless of how gifted they might be, as amateurs.

MacGregor was one of the top pros in his profession. In fact, he was *the* top pro, having succeeded in assassinating the former top pro, which entitled him to command the highest fees in the guild. However, since Mac was an equal opportunity assassin, he often used a sliding scale, for the benefit of those who couldn't afford his regular rates. Every now and then, someone came along who really needed killing, and Mac figured it would be a shame to let people like that live simply because their victims could not afford his rates.

In this particular case, though, he was getting his top rate, plus an attractive bonus, and he didn't even have to kill anyone. All he had to do was find three individuals and deliver them to Warrick the White. The problem was, he didn't really know who these individuals were. All he had was a general description. One was tall and lean, with brown hair and a long face. One was short and stocky, balding, with a long fringe of light brown hair. And one was of medium height, slim, with red hair and a beard, and he never spoke. Or, perhaps, he very seldom spoke. Granted, this wasn't much to go on, but Mac knew that the three of them had been together, and were possibly thieves, and they had last been seen at this cottage, where they had delivered a certain apparatus of unknown and possibly magical properties, which they had brought here in a horse-drawn cart and sold to Blackrune 4.

This still wasn't much in the way of information, but then that was the reason for the attractive bonus. If these three had been easy to find, anyone could have done it. Then there was the fact of Blackrune 4's mysterious disappearance, and that of his apprentice, as well. MacGregor did not know the reason for these disappearances, but the fact that a sorcerer and his apprentice had vanished without trace shortly after encountering these three suggested that there might be a certain element of danger involved in this assignment. However, Mac liked danger. Almost as much as he liked attractive bonuses.

"Look about the grounds," he said to the brothers. "And inspect the area nearby."

"What are we seeking?" one of them asked.

"Anything out of the ordinary," Mac replied. " 'Tis an isolated place, this. It does not have the look of a place that gets many visitors. See what you can find."

"This is no work for assassins," the youngest of the three brothers said irritably. "Skulking about and seeking things, 'tis work for footpads!"

"You are not assassins yet, Hugh," Mac reminded them, "but merely apprentice henchmen. If you wish to be professional assassins, you must learn your trade from the ground up. There is more to assassination than simply coming up to somebody and killing them. You must first learn to stalk your target, and to stalk him, you must first *find* him. So, go and start looking. See if our targets have left any traces of their visit."

"Suppose we find no traces?" the middle brother asked.

"Well, now, suppose you don't, Dugh," Mac said. "What would be your next step, do you think?"

Dugh frowned in concentration.

"Lugh?" said Mac, turning to the oldest brother.

"Follow that road there and attempt to retrace their

route," said Lugh. "Perhaps we may find some local people on the way who might have seen them."

"Very good, Lugh," Mac said. "You're coming along nicely. Now, why couldn't you have thought of that, Dugh?"

"I'm sorry, Mac," said Dugh, shuffling his foot on the ground.

"Aye, well, next time, you'll know better," Mac said. "Now go and have a look around."

As the three brothers split up to look around the area, Mac sat down on a tree stump and idly flipped one of his knives. Hugh, Dugh, and Lugh were actually pretty decent henchmen, he thought, fierce and deadly fighters, if a trifle overeager. A little bit of seasoning and they'd make excellent assassins.

He had found them in a Pittsburgh tavern called The Stealers, a popular gathering spot for pickpockets, cutpurses, and alleymen (the term "muggers" not having been coined yet). They were the only ones left standing after a brawl that had involved most of the patrons. It was a brawl that had started when the ticklish Dugh had discovered a stealthy hand in each of his pockets and realized that he was being simultaneously dipped by two different thieves. One was bad enough, but two was simply intolerable and Dugh had taken serious exception to this rudeness. His two brothers had joined him in the ensuing fight, while all the other patrons of the tavern, save for a wench or two, had joined the opposition.

It had been no contest. Mac had dropped in for a drink, mere moments after it was over, and was confronted by the sight of limp bodies lying all about the room, under overturned tables and draped over the bar, and in the middle of it all stood the three strapping, bruised and bloody brothers with great big grins on their simple peasant faces.

"You three did all this by yourselves?" he'd asked, and

when they'd started for him, Mac had raised his hands and said, "Nay, not me, lads. I just came in for a drink and I'd be honored if you'd join me. Though it appears we shall have to pour our own."

He'd recruited them right then and there. Mac enjoyed helping out talented young people and giving them a leg up. He had been fortunate in his own career and this was merely his way of giving something back.

"Mac! Over here! I think I've found something!"

It was Dugh. Mac hurried toward the sound of his voice. By the time he got there, Dugh's two brothers had already joined him. Dugh was standing underneath some trees behind a hedgerow at the edge of the meadow.

"What have you found?" asked Mac.

"A wee wooden horse," said Dugh in a puzzled tone, staring at something he was clutching in his hand.

Mac held his hand out and Dugh dropped a handmade wooden chesspiece into his palm. "'Tis a knight," said Mac.

"Don't look nothing like a knight," said Hugh. "Looks like a horse, to me."

"Nay, 'tis called a knight, I tell you," Mac replied. "'Tis a chesspiece."

"A what?" said Lugh.

"A chesspiece. 'Tis a game one plays with a checkered board and little wooden figures carved in different shapes. Kings, queens, bishops . . . this one is called a knight."

"Why is it called a knight if it looks like a horse?" asked Dugh.

"Because a knight rides upon a horse, I suppose," said Mac.

"Why not carve a knight, then?" Hugh asked.

"Because a horse is merely used to represent the knight," Mac explained.

"Do they carve a throne to represent the king?" asked Lugh.

"Nay, they carve a king."

"Then why not carve a knight, then? I don't see the point."

Mac rolled his eyes. "Never mind. 'Tis not important." He glanced around. "Tell me what else you can see here."

The brothers looked around.

"Wagon tracks," said Hugh.

"Very good," Mac replied. "And what can we discern about these wagon tracks? Look closely, now."

"They're deep," said Lugh.

"And what does this tell us?"

" 'Twas something heavy in the wagon."

"Good. Very good. What else?"

"Footprints," Dugh said, pointing.

"Aye. What about them?"

"Ground must've been damp when they was made," said Hugh.

"Aside from that."

"They're different sizes," Lugh said, bending down to examine them more closely.

"Which means how many men?" Mac prompted him.

"Two," said Dugh.

"Nay, three," his brother Hugh corrected him.

"Excellent," said Mac, clapping them each on the shoulder. "We know that they were here, then."

"Well, we *already* knew *that*," said Lugh.

"Nay, we had merely been told that," Mac said. "Now we know for certain. One must never take such things for granted. Remember, when you stalk someone, you must make certain of all your information for yourself. That way, you know you have the *correct* information. So now we know that three men with a loaded wagon were here, and that at least two of them play chess, for it takes two to play the game and one would not likely bring it along if he was the only one of the three who played."

"Is it important, about the chess?" asked Dugh.

" 'Tis one more thing we know about those whom we seek," said Mac. "Each thing we learn shall make finding them a little easier."

"S'trewth, you sure are clever, Mac," Hugh said with admiration.

" 'Tis merely experience, lads."

"I wish *we* could have experience, too!" said Dugh.

Mac sighed. "We're working on it, lads. We're working on it."

". . . so, there you have it," Brewster said. "Unless I can find that missing time machine, I'll never be able to get home. The trouble is, I have no way of knowing if it's here. It was programmed the same way the second one was, the one that brought me here, but there's been no sign of it and no one around here seems to know anything about it. I have to proceed on the assumption that it's here somewhere, for the alternative is simply too unnerving to contemplate. Perhaps the emergency chute opened and it was carried farther by the wind. Maybe it came down in the forest somewhere and no one's spotted it yet. But one way or another, somehow I *have* to find it. Otherwise . . ." Brewster's voice trailed off.

"Well, that certainly is quite a story," said the dragon. "It seems you have quite a problem on your hands. Perhaps there is something I can do to help."

"You think so?" said Brewster.

"I could keep an eye out for this machine of yours," said Rory. "Perhaps I will be able to spot it from the sky. Dragons have remarkable vision, you know."

"Oh, if you only could," said Brewster. "I would be very grateful."

"I shall expect something in return," said Rory.

"Whatever I can do," said Brewster.

"You can tell me more stories," said the dragon.

"Stories?"

"About your dimension, the world you came from," Rory said. "There are some things I have seen in dreams that I do not completely understand. Perhaps you could explain them to me."

"That's all?" asked Brewster.

"To a dragon, a good tale is more precious than any treasure," Rory said. "A tale is like a waking dream, and dreams are the roots of hope and wisdom. I will fly over the forest and search for your machine. And in return, you shall tell me tales of your world. Is it a bargain?"

"It's a deal," said Brewster, holding out his hand without thinking.

Rory reached out with a huge, curved talon and gently touched his hand. Brewster stared at it and swallowed hard.

"I shall speak with the fairies, too," said Rory, "and ask them to help me look. If your machine is out there, we shall find it. But you must promise not to leave till I have had my fill of stories."

"I promise," Brewster said.

"Excellent," the dragon said. "Excellent, indeed. I will look forward to it. We can begin tomorrow night."

And with that, the dragon spread its wings and plummeted off the tower. It came up again in a large and graceful arc, beat its wings, and soared up into the sky, receding rapidly into the distance until it was no more than a faint dot high up in the clouds.

"Amazing," Brewster said with awe. "Truly amazing! I

can hardly believe it. I've actually met a *dragon*, and spoken with it! Isn't it wonderful, Mick?''

"Perhaps 'tis *not* so wonderful," said Mick.

"What, are you kidding? Why?''

"You made a promise to the dragon," Mick replied. "You made a bargain with it."

"So? What's wrong with that? I fully intend to live up to it. All I have to do is answer some questions and tell some stories. What's so hard about that?''

"You promised not to leave until it's had its fill of tales," Mick replied. "Dragons dearly do love tales, y'know. They can never get enough o' them."

"Well, so I'll stay a little longer," Brewster said. "This is an incredible world, Mick, and I've barely even scratched the surface of it! There's so much to discover, so much to *learn* . . . it could take years!''

"It could take forever," Mick replied.

"Forever?''

"Aye. That's how long dragons live."

"Dragons live *forever?*"

"Aye. Forever. And they love tales even more than they love to frolic in the autumn mist," said Mick. He grinned and patted the chamberpot. "We may as well help our new friend get good and settled, Brian. It looks as if he might be stayin' for a spell, no pun intended."

And so, as Brewster considers the fact that one of the disadvantages of a verbal agreement is that you can't read the fine print, we take our leave of the reluctant sorcerer, but only for a short while, because strange and nefarious new developments are afoot.

The plans for the production of the "many-bladed knife" are about to see fruition, and as soon as Mick is finished with the molds, the first Swiss Army knives will appear in the Land of Darn and find their way into the hands of itinerant traders, which will cause Brewster more trouble than he could ever imagine.

The innocent introduction of technology, however primitive, will bring about significant changes not only at the keep, but at Brigand's Roost, as well. And despite Brewster's efforts at keeping a low profile, his reputation will gradually spread and cause ripples of gossip that will eventually reach all the way to Pittsburgh.

And as the three brigands, Long Bill, Fifer Bob, and Silent Fred, nervously maintain their silence about the missing time machine, they remain unaware that they are being stalked by the fearsome Mac the Knife and his three apprentice henchmen, the brawling brothers Hugh, Dugh, and Lugh, who have been sent out on their mission by the most powerful sorcerer in all the twenty-seven kingdoms.

Will the bumbling brigands be able to protect Brewster? For that matter, will they be able to protect themselves? Will the beautiful Black Shannon finally meet her match in the handsome Sean MacGregor? Will Brewster find a way to help Prince Brian, or will the werepot prince be doomed to his enchantment for all time? Will Warrick Morgannan, the evil Grand Director of the Sorcerers and Adepts Guild, penetrate the mysteries of Brewster's time machine, or will he continue to give the narrator a lot of grief?

"I *heard* that," said Warrick, looking up from his massive desk while he perused his ancient scrolls.

And what about poor, seductive Pamela? Join us again for our next exciting and bizarre adventure, *The Inadequate Adept*, or The Pittsburgh Stealers.

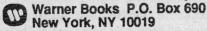